OPERATION WOLF HUNT

I0598607

STEPHEN ROSS

BLACK PARROT BOOKS
San Diego, California

To everyone who has suffered the devastation caused by drugs.

Always to E and A.

The war on drugs was an ideology the government came up with, and there never really was a war on drugs. I mean, to stop the importation of drugs into the United States of America is an impossibility.

~ George Jung

When you actually study the beginnings of the federal war on drugs, you uncover a history of lies, bigotry, and ignorance so extensive it will leave you speechless.

~ Ron Paul

The war on drugs has failed in West Africa and around the world.

~ Kofi Annan

1

SUN RAYS DANCED on the harbor as soft clouds began their march over the tip of Point Loma. A gentle breeze carried gulls in its arms, and a destroyer cruised beneath the span, trailing its carrier like a shadow. The Silver Strand swept to the south and kept the ocean at bay, pointing the way to Imperial Beach and Tijuana beyond.

The Coronado Bridge hummed with usual traffic, but it was a bittersweet crossing for Luke. He'd spent the past ten years eating, breathing, training, and deploying as a Navy SEAL. Most of it as a sniper. Not just any sniper, but the best there was—nobody could match him. And today was it. He was saying goodbye to start a new life back home in the small town of Cedar Bend, Colorado.

The decision to leave was difficult. Luke loved being a SEAL, the mental and physical challenge, camaraderie, and satisfaction that comes from being good at what you do. But at thirty-eight, he didn't know how much longer he could keep up the pace required of an active duty sniper. And he had no interest in desk work or instructing others. He wanted to leave of his own accord, at the top of his game, and not be gently nudged out to pasture.

He drove down Orange Avenue and through a flood of memories. Danny's Palm Bar & Grill looked sleepy in the morning light with the neon palm turned off and no inebriated late-nighters hanging out on the sidewalk, bragging about doing this and that. Two blocks farther, McP's Irish Pub suffered the same morning fate. Nighttime was when these places came alive, and the SEALs rolled in to relieve job stress and bond.

Oh, the times! Not the drunken kind, the sober kind. Luke was a one-beer-a-night guy, but he usually had more fun than everyone else. He'd rescued more than one buddy from an altercation over some alcohol-induced threat or ill-spoken reference about a sister. Those times would be missed, and he wondered about civilian life. Could he adjust to less-structured living, to the small town where he grew up, to the ghost of an abusive father lurking around every corner? He'd know soon enough.

As he was waved through the gate at Naval Amphibious Base Coronado, Luke saw the long, green lawn where he'd graduated from BUD/S training all those years ago. Such a proud moment. His mom sat beaming, and his dad was sober, at least he appeared to be. That day marked the beginning of many exciting, challenging, and action-packed years. No regrets. None.

He parked in front of the Naval Special Warfare Center and sat looking at the building. This was it. The last stop before heading home to Colorado. It was the most difficult of the goodbyes. Admiral Becker was more than Luke's commander. He was a friend, a mentor, and the father Luke wished he'd had.

The Center interior was plain, giving no indication it housed the command for the most skilled fighting force in the world. Luke stopped in front of Admiral Becker's door, took a breath, and knocked.

"Come in."

Luke opened the door. The two men looked at one

another, each wearing the hint of a smile.

"Good morning, sir." Luke snapped a salute.

"Oh, stop with the sir. We're friends, Luke. And you're no longer under my command as of today."

"Yes, sir, uh, Admiral."

The admiral got up and embraced Luke. "And stop with the Admiral too. It's, Tom. Got it?"

"Hooyah."

The admiral walked back to his desk and motioned for Luke to have a seat. "We're going to miss you around here, Luke. You're our best. You know that."

"Thank you, sir, uh, Tom."

Admiral Becker smiled. "So, what are your plans? I hear you're moving back to Colorado."

"I am, but other than moving, I have no plans. I've thought about starting a survival school. It's something I've been interested in since I was a kid, and I could continue to use my SEAL training."

"I'm sure you'd be great at it. If you're ever not satisfied on the outside, you can always come back. We'd love to have you as an instructor."

"Thanks, Tom. I appreciate that. I don't know if I'd be happy teaching. I like the challenge of doing."

"I understand. But know the offer remains open."

A voice came on the intercom. "Excuse me, Admiral. Captain Benson is here."

"Thank you, Helen. Send him back."

Luke stood, his eyes scanning the office, and said, "I'm going to miss you, Tom."

"And I, you. Stay in touch, Luke."

They exchanged salutes as Luke let out a "Hooyah" and left.

2

LUKE SCANNED DOWNTOWN San Diego as he made his way back over the bridge. He wondered when he'd see it again, if ever. San Diego had been his oasis between long tours in the Middle East. It was his favorite duty station: perfect weather, beautiful beaches, mountains, and desert solitude all in one county.

The new Jeep Wrangler felt solid as it turned onto I-8 east and headed toward the mountains. Luke had never owned a vehicle. He'd been frugal and saved all he could, sending a few dollars home to his mom for emergencies. The jeep was a gift to himself. A reward for all the sweat over the past twenty years. It was perfect for Colorado's mountains and snowy winters.

As he dropped into the desert and passed Ocotillo, flashbacks of Afghanistan played on his mind. The Anza-Borrego Desert wasn't much different from the Registan Desert outside Kandahar. True, he didn't see any camels, turbaned warriors, or donkeys pulling carts; but the geography looked the same.

It was in the mountains of the Registan that Luke took out his most distant target: the top Taliban commander in the region. Luke and his spotter, Chuck Reagan, had blended with the rock and dirt for four days, eyes glued to the spotting scope, before the beard they were waiting for came into view. An old pickup stopped next to a low stone building, and the target got out. Several men armed with AK-47s walked up to greet him and stood talking in front of the truck, oblivious to the awaiting death.

Chuck was an ace at estimating distance and calling wind, and the Garrett/Reagan team had the shot dialed in within seconds. Luke let out a breath and slowly squeezed the trigger. After a quick beat, the target dropped. The other men crouched and looked around, trying to determine where the shot had come from. Confusion reigned below as Luke and Chuck retrieved all evidence of their presence, slipped into a ravine, and jogged to safety. The target had been taken at a distance of 2.31 miles. The longest known kill, ever.

Luke turned north at Gila Bend on his way through the Sonoran Desert, passed Buckeye, and on to Surprise, Arizona, for a late lunch. Kenchuto, a Buddhist word meaning being absolutely natural, was Luke's favorite vegan restaurant. He'd eaten there as a kid on his first trip to California. The food was tasty, and because his mom embraced veganism with a passion, so did Luke. He'd taken some flack for his eating habits during the first few weeks of BUD/S training, especially from the Midwest meat-and-potato guys. The term "pussy" had been tossed his way more than once. But that ended when he proved himself to be the top dog in class.

Back on the road, Luke headed to Flagstaff for a reunion with his buddy, Chuck Reagan. If traffic held, he should be there by 6:00 p.m. Chuck completed his Navy contract and had been living in Arizona for the past three months. Luke was eager to talk with him about his adjustment to civilian life.

As Luke pulled into the driveway, he spotted Chuck sitting on the porch wearing khaki shorts and flip-flops, waving a Corona, and flashing his easy, white smile.

Chuck said, "Hey, man, good to see you," as he

walked to the jeep.

Luke gave Chuck a hug and said, "You too. It's been awhile. How you doin'?"

"Oh, you know. It's different. Takes some getting used to, but it's good. I like it." Then he turned toward the house and said, "Come on, let me grab you a beer, and we'll catch up."

"Sounds good. Man, it's hot out here."

The bottles clinked together as Chuck said, "Salud. Welcome, my friend."

"Thanks. Salud back at ya."

Both men took the customary drink, and Luke said, "So, do you miss it? What do you do with yourself now?"

"Yeah, sometimes I miss it. You don't find that kind of action here in Flagstaff or anywhere else for that matter. But I stay active. I workout, run every day, and shoot at the range once a week. And if you promise not to tell any of the guys ... promise?

"Sure."

"I'm working at my girlfriend's flower shop. Arranging bouquets, mostly."

Luke smiled and said, "That's sweet," as Chuck's eyebrows shot up. "No, really, I think it's nice for a man to get in touch with his feminine side," then squinting and leaning closer, he said, "Are you wearing eyeshadow?"

Chuck's fist connected with Luke's shoulder as he laughed and said, "Yeah. Want some?"

"I'll pass. Thanks."

Chuck's expression changed, and he said, "Does what we did ever bother you? I mean, a hundred eighty-one confirmed kills. That's a lot."

"Yeah, it is. At first, I wondered how it would affect

me. But it's never bothered me. I believe there are greedy, egomaniacal, evil people who refuse to conform to the norms of human decency. The only way to deal with them is to eliminate them. Think about the many lives saved and the unimaginable suffering prevented by the elimination of one such person. I know there are lots of people who disagree. But based on my life experience, that's my belief."

"That's how I feel. I thought it should bother me, but it doesn't." Then changing the subject, Chuck said, "Hey, guess what! I'm a vegan!

"No way. Good for you, man. What changed your mind?"

"You did. After watching you all those years and seeing you at the top of your game, I thought, what the hell, give it a go. I haven't had meat, eggs, dairy, or processed food in six weeks."

"Awesome!"

"And you were right. I do have more energy. I feel stronger and don't get tired in the middle of the day."

"Told ya."

"Hey, speaking of that, how about I whip us up some ginger veggie stir-fry?

"Let's do it. And wipe that eyeshadow off."

Luke was up at 6:00 a.m., and Chuck already had coffee made. They sat at the kitchen table drinking coffee, reliving the past ten years they'd worked together, and discussing the future. After a brotherly hug and agreeing to stay in touch, Luke hit the road.

3

THE DRIVE INTO Cedar Bend hadn't changed as long as Luke could remember. The road traversed mountains and descended into valleys where aspen, fir, and pine lined the way while Ute Creek burbled its gentle welcome. Although sorry to be leaving the SEALs, Luke was looking forward to spending time with his mom and exploring the wilderness he'd grown to love as a kid. His alcoholic dad had been gone for nine months, the result of a burned-out liver. So there wouldn't be any more late-night trips to the police station or worrying about his mom's safety. Maybe it would be a welcome change from the rigors of the past several years.

A smile crossed Luke's mouth as he approached the main intersection in town. A large banner strung across the street read WELCOME HOME LUKE GARRETT. He'd called his mom from Flagstaff before he left to give her his ETA. She was standing on the corner wearing a clown suit, jumping up and down, and waving her arms. Leave it to Dorothy Garrett. She was full of spirit. Numerous other people he recognized stood around her, clapping.

Luke pulled over and got out to greet his mom. She locked him in a bear hug as joyous tears wet her cheeks, and a chorus of voices shouted: "Welcome back, Luke." "Good to see you, buddy." "Thanks for your service."

The crowd dissipated, and Luke drove his mom home.

He spent the first few weeks catching up with his mom and helping around the house, mowing the lawn, painting the porch, fixing a plumbing leak, and running errands. He connected with the few high school friends who'd stuck around; most of whom were married with kids. They were good people but not very worldly. Their conversations were driven by local gossip. Luke found he no longer had much in common with them.

Turner's Cafe had been in business for forty-five years and was Cedar Bend's favorite eatery. It had been closed for two years since old man Turner served his last meal and passed to the other side while tallying the day's receipts. It was in the heart of town and was the perfect place for Luke to open a survival school. In addition to the spacious front area, it had a kitchen and a large back office that could be turned into a bedroom.

Luke made Mrs. Turner's day when he gave her a hefty down payment and bought the building. She carried paper on the balance that would provide her with additional income for the next five years. A carpenter friend helped remodel the interior, and Luke set about outlining the courses he hoped to offer. His first clients were the local boy scouts who signed up for a weeklong course on survival in the mountains. He worked pro bono, and the scouts took out an ad in the local paper promoting the business. The Out There survival school was born.

Like most new businesses, Out There started slow. A husband and wife from Atlanta were Luke's first paying clients. They were visiting relatives in town and wanted to learn how to survive in the wild. It was nice to know he could make money doing what he loved.

Luke hadn't done any advertising other than the sign that hung out front, so business was limited to locals and folks from nearby towns.

Then came the call that changed it all.

It had been a quiet week, and Luke was working on the syllabus for an edible wild plants course he planned to offer when his cell phone rang. "This is Luke."

"Luke, it's Tom. How the heck are you?"

"Admiral! What a great surprise. I'm fine. How are you?"

"I'm doing well. I heard you started your survival business. How's it going?"

"Slow. But I haven't done much promotion. I'm trying to get the courses nailed down first."

"Good for you." There was a pause and audible throat clearing before Admiral Becker continued. "Luke, somethings come up, and I'd like to get you on board. Chuck Reagan too."

Luke laughed. "Is this an attempt to get me to re-up?"

"No, no. It's much bigger than that." The Admiral sounded serious. "I can't discuss it on the phone. Any chance you can get down here Wednesday morning? I wouldn't ask if it wasn't important."

"Uh, I guess."

"Great. I'm gonna call Chuck as soon as we hang up. Flying out of Flagstaff is probably the easiest. Maybe the two of you can fly in together. And don't worry about expenses. You'll be reimbursed for everything."

"OK."

Continuing, Admiral Becker said, "It would be best if you don't tell anyone about this call or where you're going. Make something up. Tell people you're going to visit a friend."

With hesitation in his voice, Luke said, "I got it."

"Let me know when your arrival is confirmed. I'll have a car waiting for you, and come straight to my office when you get in."

"Will do."

"I'll see you soon. Good talking to you, Luke."

"Yes, sir. Good talking with you too. I think."

The connection went dead, and Luke's forehead furrowed in thought. He knew this had something to do with his past service because the Admiral wanted Reagan involved too. But what? Luke was enjoying small town life, things were going well, and he wasn't sure he wanted to return to the past. It was over. Time to move on.

Luke tried to focus on the course outline he'd been preparing, but the concentration wasn't there. He gave Chuck a call before heading to his mom's for dinner. Although Chuck was uncertain about going, they made plans for Luke to stay in Flagstaff on Tuesday night, then fly to San Diego together Wednesday morning.

4

CORONADO ISLAND, AND the building where Luke said goodbye to Admiral Becker four months earlier, came into view just before the plane passed by the skyscrapers of San Diego and landed at what used to be known as Lindbergh Field, now San Diego International Airport. So much for the memory of Lucky Lindy. The plane taxied to the gate on schedule, and ten minutes later Luke and Chuck approached a Navy uniform holding a sign bearing their names.

"Chief Garrett, Petty Officer Reagan, welcome to San Diego."

Luke extended his hand and said, "Thank you, Seaman Jones. But drop the Chief. I'm a civilian now, and it's Luke."

Chuck put out a hand and said, "That goes for Petty Officer too. Thanks for picking us up."

"My pleasure. Follow me gentlemen, and I'll take you to the base. Admiral Becker is anxious to see you."

Pulling out of the airport, Luke spotted the U.S.S. *Abraham Lincoln* docked at North Island.

"Hey, Chuck. Stink'n Lincoln's in port. I wonder if Bernie Taub is in town. I haven't seen him in three years."

"Me neither. Last I heard he was in Kandahar. But that was over a year ago. If I know Taub, he's probably shacked up with some exotic babe in a mud hut somewhere. That guy sure had a way with the ladies."

"That he did. I'll shake the trees while we're here and see if he falls out. It would be great to see him again. We had some good times back in the day."

"True that."

The car continued through town, onto the 5 freeway, and over the Coronado Bridge to the base. As they came to a stop in front of the Naval Special Warfare Center, Chuck said, "So, what if the Admiral asks us to come back?"

"I don't know. I'm happy back home in Colorado and really not interested in getting back into the fray. But let's see what he has to say."

An airconditioned breeze brushed away the summer heat as Jones opened the Warfare Center door. Admiral Becker was there to greet them, and in his gravelly voice, said, "Luke, Chuck, thanks for coming. Great to see you guys again. How's the civilian world treating you?"

Luke said, "I can't complain. It's nice to be back home in the mountains."

"That goes for me too, sir."

"Well, I'm glad to hear it. But enough small talk. Let's get down to why I asked you to come. Follow me."

Luke and Chuck exchanged looks and fell into step behind the Admiral. They entered his office and saw a man they'd never seen before, dressed in civilian clothes, and sitting on a sofa facing the door. He was a few pounds overweight, bald on top, sporting a pair of designer sunglasses, and bearing a noticeable scar that ran from his left eyebrow to the corner of his mouth. A mouth with paper-thin lips supporting a John Waters-type mustache. As the man rose, Admiral Becker said, "Luke, Chuck, this is Dan Colby of the CIA. He asked me to bring you here today, so he can brief you on a proposal the CIA has for your services."

"Gentlemen, thank you for coming. I've heard great things about you two, and it's a pleasure to finally meet you."

The hand Colby raised was missing most of the ring and pinky fingers, a fact that made Luke wonder about his involvement with the CIA. Luke took the hand and found its grip strong despite the digit shortage and said, "Nice to meet you, sir."

As Chuck shook Colby's hand, Admiral Becker said, "Dan is not here on Navy business. This is strictly a CIA affair and doesn't involve me or the SEALs. He asked that your meeting be private, so I reserved the conference room at the end of the hall for you. Water and coffee are on the credenza. Give me a buzz if you need anything else." Addressing Luke and Chuck, he said, "I know you've got a flight back home this afternoon, but stop by before you leave."

Luke said, "Will do."

Admiral Becker pointed to his door and said, "Gentlemen, the conference room is to your right."

The three men walked in silence down the hall to the conference room. Once inside, Colby closed the door, sat at the head of the conference table, and said, "Please, sit."

The room was silent except for the barely perceptible push of air through the overhead vents. Colby was quiet as he studied the men with the unsettling steely scrutiny he'd developed during his years as a top CIA foreign operative. He finally spoke in a voice tainted by cigarettes, lots of cigarettes, and said, "I don't have to tell you that you're the best at what you do."

Luke interjected and said, "Did, sir. We don't do that anymore."

"Yes, I understand. But your skill is still there. It can

be brought back, kept sharp, and used for the good of your country and the world at large. Gentlemen, the CIA needs your services."

Luke said, Thank you for your confidence in us, sir. But as for me, I'm retired and living a quiet life back in Colorado doing what I love to do. I've put that past life behind me."

Chuck said, "Me too. I'm retired and enjoying a life free from the stress of war. I can't see going back."

"Have you men heard of Carlos Quintana, also known as El Lobo?" Both men nodded. "Quintana is the most notorious, vile drug lord in the world today. He is known to have personally tortured and executed more than one hundred people, including women and children. His Colima Cartel has distributed tons of heroin, cocaine, and meth throughout the United States and the world. It is responsible for the death of hundreds of thousands of people, and the suffering of millions of others. Mexico has tried to stop him, but too many corrupt politicians, police, and military personnel have stood in the way. The United States can stop him—you can stop him."

Luke said, "Sir, with all due respect, I have no desire to join the CIA."

"That's not what I'm suggesting. You both have found a good life outside of the military. I respect that and am not asking you to give it up, only to consider occasionally setting it aside for short periods of time for the greater good. You wouldn't be part of the CIA, only independent contractors."

Luke said, "Define 'occasionally' and 'short periods of time' for me."

"Sure. You'd get an assignment once, twice, maybe three times a year. Each assignment lasting from a few days to a few weeks. We have training ranges around the country that would be available to you at your request. We'd provide any equipment you need, all your expenses would be covered, and you'd each receive two hundred fifty thousand dollars per contract."

Chuck said, "That's a lot of money."

"It is. But a drop in the bucket compared to the hundreds of millions of dollars Quintana and his thugs cost the US alone every year. And Quintana is just one of many evil people scattered around the world that wreak havoc on innocent people every day."

Luke said, "Don't you have people inside your organization that can do the job?"

"Yes. We do. But there is no one as skilled and efficient as the two of you. I wouldn't be here if we didn't need you. Gentlemen, I'm not asking you to decide right now. I wanted to give you an overview of the operation and answer your questions. Then you can take some time before giving me your answer. Please, think about it, talk to one another, call me if you have questions, and be prepared to give me your answer one week from today. Quintana has a ranch in the Sierra Madre mountains in Sonora, Mexico, about sixty miles south of the border. Our intel says he'll be there in one month for about two weeks. That gives us a great window of opportunity that doesn't happen often."

Luke took a moment to process what he'd just heard and said, "It's an interesting proposal. No guarantees, but I'll think about it. Chuck would have to be on board for me to do it."

"That goes for me too. I wouldn't do it without Luke."

"Of course. We want you as a team. Just so you know, this is an arrangement of mutual trust. There will be no written contracts. I will be your only contact with the agency, and you may stop taking assignments at any time. However, once you agree to a mission you must see it through to the end.

Luke and Chuck nodded their understanding.

Colby wrote some numbers on a piece of paper and slid it across the table to Luke. "This is my direct line at Langley. Both of you memorize it and then destroy the paper. Call me if you have any questions, and I'll contact you both in a week for your answer. If we have a deal, you'll be flown to Langley on the sixteenth." Colby reached inside his briefcase, pulled out two cell phones, and passed them across the table. "These phones are encrypted. Use them only to communicate with me and each other. Even though they're encrypted, don't mention any specific names, places, dates, or times when using them. Oh, and this meeting never happened."

Colby rose, picked up his briefcase, and said, "Gentlemen, it's been a pleasure. I look forward to working with you." He did an about-face and left the room.

Luke and Chuck exchanged looks, got up, walked down the hall in silence, did a brief catch-up with Admiral Becker, and forgetting all about trying to contact their friend, Bernie Taub, flew home.

5

THE DAYS PASSED like any other week. Luke continued outlining survival course plans, had dinners with his mom, and took a group from a local backpacking club on a three-day edible plant identification trip. Chuck jogged his five miles a day and helped his girlfriend arrange flowers.

On Friday, Luke gave Chuck a call. "Hey, man, how're things?"

"Luke, thanks for calling. Good to hear from you. I was thinking about giving you a call today. So, have you made a decision?"

"That's why I'm calling. I want to get your thoughts. But, yeah, I'm leaning toward doing it."

"Great. Me too."

Chuck, I keep going over what C said about Q. That man is pure evil. He shouldn't be allowed to keep on causing so much death and destruction and ruining the lives of so many innocent people. If we can stop him, I believe we have an obligation to do it."

"My thoughts exactly. We need to give it a go."

"So, we're doin' it?"

"Yeah."

"You know someone's gonna step up and replace Q?"

"No doubt. But, hey, more work for us."

"That's sick."

"I know. Perhaps if we do our job well, they'll eventually get the hint that that line of work isn't healthy. Who knows?"

"That would be the best outcome. But it's doubtful because there's too much money to be had. C should call tomorrow, so let's talk again after we hear what he has to say."

"Ten-four. See ya."

"Adios."

Luke's encrypted phone rang at 9:00 a.m. the next morning. He knew who was calling and answered. "Yes?"

A smoky voice said, "Is that your answer?"

"Yes."

"Good. I knew it would be."

"And how is that?"

"Because a part of you misses the action, the adrenaline rush, the feeling that comes from knowing you've stopped evil and prevented suffering."

Colby was right. He did miss those things. Especially the part about stopping evil and preventing suffering.

"So what's next?"

"Pack light and be at the Durango-La Plata County Airport at 10:00 a.m. on the date previously mentioned. We'll pick up your friend and be back at my office in time for a cocktail before dinner."

"OK."

"You're doing the right thing. Welcome aboard."

6

A SHINY GULFSTREAM jet was parked on the apron of the Durango airport when Luke arrived. His mom had driven him the sixty miles from Cedar Bend and now sat staring at him. Worry lines creased her forehead.

"Mom, I'll be OK."

Her eyes filling with tears, Dorothy said, "I know, but I worry just the same. I know you're off to do something dangerous. I can tell. You're always more serious."

Luke leaned over, kissed her on the cheek, and held her in his arms. "I love you, mom. I'll be back in a few weeks." He got out of the car, grabbed his duffel bag, and headed to the terminal, stopping long enough to give his mom a wave.

Colby was waiting when the terminal doors opened. He wore the same sober expression he had when they met in San Diego. Luke wondered if the guy ever smiled. Probably not. A partially-fingered hand was thrust at Luke as his CIA contact said, "Good to see you. Follow me."

The interior of the jet was elegant. The nicest Luke had ever seen. Of course, he'd only been in military planes and commercial airliners, never a private jet. Colby pointed to a seat near the front and took the seat facing it. An attractive flight attendant approached and asked if there was anything she could get for them. Both men declined, and an hour later Chuck stepped on board. The flight to Langley was quick and uneventful. The men engaged in small talk at first, then Colby took a nap, Chuck played with his cell phone, and Luke alternated between reading the *Washington Post*, trying to nap, and watching the mosaic-like patterns of the earth pass below. Colby woke when the plane touched down.

Colby exited the plane first, followed by Luke, then Chuck. He pointed to a six-story building to his left and said, "That's building 2110. My office is on the second floor, number 212. That five-story, brown building behind us and to the right is building 2130. That's where you'll be staying while at Langley. You can't see it from here, but the building directly behind yours is the restaurant and general store. You can get pretty much anything you want there."

Luke said, "I've been sitting too long. I think I'll go for a run and grab a shower before heading to dinner."

Chuck said he'd join him.

"Feel free to familiarize yourselves with the place, and let's plan to meet at my office in the morning at eight."

Luke said, "Sounds good. See you then."

Chuck responded with, "Later."

Luke and Chuck headed off to their dorm, and Colby walked toward his office. They each had their own room complete with a queen-sized bed, walk-in shower, desk, 32-inch HDTV, and view of the surrounding woods. Nicer than expected.

After running five miles around the complex, they showered and walked to the restaurant. It was another nice surprise, as the food was excellent. They both gave it five stars. Hunger sated, they retired to their rooms. Luke continued work on a high-altitude survival course he planned to incorporate into his list of classes, and

Chuck played solitaire. They both turned in early and were up at 6:00 a.m. in time for another run and gourmet breakfast before going to Colby's office for the initial mission briefing.

Colby opened his office door, and pointing to a distinguished gentleman wearing an expensive Armani suit, greeted them with, "Gentlemen, this is Don Hewitt, Director of the CIA."

Director Hewitt stood, shook their hands, and said, "It's a real pleasure to finally meet the two of you. I've heard great things about what you accomplished in Iraq and Afghanistan with the SEALs. I'm delighted you decided to come on board. Your skills will be a terrific asset to the CIA."

Colby interjected with, "Director Hewitt, President Mitchell, and I are the only people other than you who know about your mission. And it must stay that way for national security reasons."

Hewitt sat and directed the other men to do the same, then said, "Gentlemen, this mission is of vital importance to our country and the world at large. Stopping Quintana and his Colima Cartel is a top priority for President Mitchell. He has authorized us to provide you with whatever you need to train and successfully complete the mission. Just ask, and you'll get it. A special bank account has been set up for each of you and one hundred twenty-five thousand dollars has been deposited into each account. The other half of your fee will be deposited upon the successful completion of your mission. Agent Colby will give you your account information. You may contact me at any time should the need arise. However, the chain of communication should typically be Agent Colby, then me. You'll also be given a number for the White House and an access code that will connect you directly with President Mitchell in case of a dire emergency."

Hewitt stood and said, "With that, I'll leave so you gentlemen can get to work. Again, welcome aboard, and thank you."

Colby looked from the door back to Luke and Chuck and said, "The code name for your mission is Operation Wolf Hunt for obvious reasons. You'll be working here with me for the next week studying the logistics of the mission and learning all we know about Quintana, his operation, and Palacio de Montaña. That's the Sierra Madre mountain compound where the target will be taken. Next week you'll have access to our sniper range. It's located about a hundred miles west of here."

Luke asked, "What about equipment?"

"We've taken the liberty of gathering all the same weapons, scopes, and other equipment you used as SEALs. I assume that will be satisfactory?"

Luke said, "That'll be good."

Chuck responded with, "Great."

Colby reached for his briefcase and pulled out a stack of high-resolution photographs. "These are drone photos taken of Quintana's mountain compound and surrounding area. I've included some schematic drawings that will give you a better read on the size of buildings and the distance between various points." He retrieved a binder from the briefcase, pushed it across the table, and continued. "This one hundred twenty-five-page memo contains everything we've gathered on the target over the past two years: his habits, movements, hangouts, bodyguards, weapons, family, friends, and mistresses. And there are plenty of the latter." Take these things and memorize them over the next week. Let's meet here again tomorrow at the same time. Any questions?"

Luke said, "Not at the moment, but I'm sure I'll have some after going over these documents."

Chuck nodded in agreement.

Colby stood and said, "OK. This should keep you busy for the rest of the day. See you in the morning."

Luke picked up the binder and other documents while Chuck grabbed another muffin. They said their goodbyes and left the office.

7

IN A SMALL village in Central Mexico, a man sat duct taped to a rusted metal chair, his face bloody and bruised, his shirt soaked with sweat as blood dripped from what used to be his pinky finger. A grimace painted his face, and tears ran down his cheeks as he cried, "El Lobo, I tell you the truth. I don't know what happened to it. I swear. I just stand by the door and guard like you tell me. Then I hear a noise like something drop, and when I look, it's gone. Disappear. I don't know how."

The man standing before him wore a business suit. He wasn't a large man, maybe five foot six and a hundred thirty pounds with a shaved head and soul patch dotting the space below his lower lip. Not large. But cool, commanding, and mean. He sneered at the sniveling man, spit in his face, and swung the bat he was holding hard into the man's right knee. The sound of cracking bone mixed with shrill screams bounced off the bare, concrete block walls.

"You damn liar. You're telling me a hundred pounds of pure cocaine just vanished into thin air? Huh? Is that what you expect me to believe?"

In between sobs, the man said, "Yes. Is true. I can tell you no more. Please. I have a family."

Quintana motioned to one of the men standing against the wall to give him the gun. The man complied. Quintana pointed the gun at the man's forehead, and in a menacing voice said, "Look at me, you swine."

The man kept his head down while tears and snot

dripped on his pants. Urine soaked his crotch, ran down his leg, and puddled in his sandals. "Please, El Lobo. Please. I tell the truth."

"Look at me, damn you."

The man continued to keep his head bowed.

Quintana grabbed the man's hair and jerked his head up. Sheer terror was etched on his face. Quintana pulled the trigger. A loud bang reverberated around the room. Quintana spit on the dead man, tossed the gun back to his bodyguard, and said, "Cut off his head and send it to his widow."

8

COLBY WAS SEATED at his desk when Luke and Chuck entered the office at 8:00 a.m. on day three. "Good morning, gentlemen. I trust your first full day here was enjoyable?"

Luke said, "Yeah, if you consider reading about Quintana and his exploits enjoyable."

Chuck added, "This El Lobo guy is one sick mother. I'm surprised he hasn't been taken out long ago."

"You and many others. The Mexican Army and Federal Police have tried for years—at least the ones who aren't on Quintana's payroll or scared to death of him. The ones who have tried usually wound up dead or resigned from their jobs. He's been a source of frustration and embarrassment for the Mexican government for a log time, but they've never officially asked for our help. So, we're taking matters into our own hands to finally put a stop to that beast. And you men are the key to getting the job done."

Luke said, "Have we ever tried to get him before?"

"Yes. Once. A few years ago, he was rumored to be in Vegas at one of the lesser-known hotels. A swat team descended on the place, but he was no where to be found. Didn't appear he'd ever been there."

Luke said, "How reliable is the source that says Quintana will be at his mountain hideout during the two-week window?"

"As reliable as it gets. Our source has been inside the Colima Cartel for years. He's apparently pissed because Quintana has been mistreating him and overlooked him for several recent assignments. Everything he's told us in the past has checked out. So, yeah, we trust him."

Colby reached in his briefcase, pulled out two satellite phones, and handed them to Luke and Chuck. "These are SATCOM10 encrypted satellite phones. They were designed and built specifically for the CIA. No one else has them, and they're virtually hack-proof. They will be your sole means of communication, guidance, and documentation during the mission. They work pretty much like any smart phone. There's a two-way radio built in with a five-mile range, and the digital camera has a 24x digital zoom. Agent Johnson is our tech specialist and will meet with you tomorrow to answer any questions you may have and guide you through the basics of how these babies work."

Chuck asked, "Will we be able to contact you at any time?"

"Yes. My cell number is programmed in the contact list along with Director Hewitt's number and the number for the White House. I'll have my phone on and with me from the time you leave here until you return. Also, the encrypted GPS will allow me to know your exact location at all times."

Colby put a detailed topographic map up on the screen behind him and said, "At the end of next week our jet will fly you to Fort Wiley in Southern Arizona. From there, a stealth Black Hawk will take you to the drop zone fifteen miles north of Palacio de Montaña."

Pointing to the map, Coby said, "This map is stored on your phones, and it, along with the GOVMAP app, will be your guide from the time you're dropped until the bird picks you up."

Luke said, "According to the map, it looks like

there's a town between the drop zone and the target. What do we know about it?"

"That's Gato Grande. It got its name from the large number of pumas that inhabit the area."

Chuck said, "Oh great. That should make the adventure more exciting."

"True. It's something you'll have to keep a lookout for but shouldn't be a problem. Oh, there are some bears in those mountains too. But black bears and mountain lions scare off pretty easily."

Luke said, "Any other hazards we should be aware of?"

"The only other wildlife that could be a concern are snakes. There are a couple of rattlesnake species and coral snakes in those mountains. But again, exercising caution, they shouldn't pose a problem."

Chuck laughed and said, "I'm beginning to think two hundred fifty thousand dollars isn't enough." Then he cracked a smile and said, "Just kidding. I've lived around snakes my whole life."

Colby continued, "About three hundred people live in and around Gato Grande. The majority are hard-working farmers who despise Quintana and what he's doing. But a few support him because of the business he brings to the town. His men are known to hang out at El Granero. It's the only dive in town that supplies both cheap drinks and female companions. Because we don't know who supports him, the best advice is to avoid everyone."

Luke said, "It looks like the area is pretty heavily forested. What's there?"

"Mostly pine and oak forest. However, Palacio de Montaña is in a large grass valley. There are a few scattered trees throughout the valley and around the house, but you should have a clear line of sight from most locations.

Luke looked at the map and said, "I see the drop zone is north of the property, and we'll be approaching the back side of the house."

"Correct. The pool and cabana are located on the north side of the house, and Quintana spends a lot of his time around the pool. So that may be the best place to take him out. The good news is that forest, peaks, and gorges surround the valley, so you should be able to easily move to another location if needed.

Chuck asked, "What's his security like?"

"There are at least two guards with Quintana at all times. Two are in the house at night, Three or four are always positioned around the property. One guard mans the gun turret on top of the house and scans the surrounding area with high-powered binoculars. And a camera-equipped, armed drone does occasional sweeps of the perimeter. They all carry a Desert Eagle .50 caliber handgun and an AK-47. So they're dangerous. Oh, and the guy in the turret has a Stinger missile launcher in case of an air attack and a .50 caliber machine gun that can take out almost anything else."

Luke said, "Good to know. We'll try to not get closer than a mile and a quarter from the target. The .50 cal isn't very effective beyond that."

For the next three days, Luke and Chuck worked with Colby on the mission details. They checked out their gear, studied photos of Quintana, his wife, current mistress, and guards, planned the best approach to the target, analyzed potential escape routes, and reviewed satellite phone use with Agent Johnson.

On Sunday, they went on a ten-mile hike and checked out the area around the town of Langley.

Week two was spent at the CIA sniper range honing their skills and finalizing preparations for their departure on Saturday.

9

THE ENGINES WERE running, the stairs were descended, and the pilots were wrapping up their preflight check when Luke reached the apron where the Gulfstream G650 was waiting. Chuck and Colby were right behind him. Colby gave them a last-minute briefing before turning and heading to the passenger waiting area. Both men walked to the plane wearing camouflage fatigues and carrying their tactical assault packs and rifles. Luke shouldered his .300 Win Mag, and Chuck carried his MK 15 and a Mk14 grenade launcher. They each had an HK .45 caliber handgun on their hip.

The flight attendant secured the door, and the engines whined as the plane began to taxi to the end of the runway. Waves of jet exhaust rippled out of the engines as Luke watched the buildings roll by. He thought of his mom and silently wished her well as he did at the start of every mission.

Chuck said, "Here we go again."

"Yeah. I didn't think we'd ever be doing it again when I drove off base five months ago. But here we are."

"At least it's close and shouldn't take long."

"Hopefully. I can't wait to get back to Colorado and my business. There's something to be said for the quiet life."

"Agreed."

Cruising at forty-five thousand feet, the ride was smooth, and the plane touched down at Fort Wiley three hours after wheels up. A Sikorsky Black Hawk was waiting on the helipad with the pilot and copilot at the controls when Luke stepped off the plane. Chuck followed, and they walked directly to the aircraft. The pilot gave a wave, and they gave one back.

Both men climbed on board as the blades started to turn. They took their seats, strapped in, and put on their headphones. The bird had been cocked, so it only took sixty seconds from rumps in seats to skids in sky.

The pilot came on and said, "Good morning, gentlemen. I'm Agent Donnelly, and my copilot is Agent Gomez.

Both Luke and Chuck said, "Good morning."

"We'll be flying you to the drop zone in a remote location of the Sonora mountains about seventy miles from here. We'll be flying low and sticking to the canyons and valleys as much as possible to avoid detection. Should be about a thirty-minute trip. You set?"

Luke said, "Ready."

Chuck responded with, "Let's rock 'n' roll."

Miniature dust devils twirled and danced at the edge of the helipad as the bird lifted. A black-tailed jack rabbit scurried to safety as the aircraft banked left and headed toward the Mexican boarder. About ten minutes into the flight, the aircraft entered a narrow, granite-walled canyon that zigged and zagged and took them higher up the mountain.

Chuck gave a forced laugh and said, "I'm glad you know what you're doing. There isn't much room for error in here."

Donnelly said, "I don't. This is my first solo flight." After an appropriately long pause, he continued, "Just kidding. I've been doing this for years. Got to fly in lots of these tight spaces in Afghanistan."

Chuck said, "You're a funny guy, Donnelly."

"I know. It's a gift. Runs in the family."

They lifted out of the canyon, crested the peak of the mountain, and descended into a long, broad valley surrounded by pine and oak trees, staying about thirty feet above the ground.

A thin man wearing a baggy white shirt and pants was walking a donkey on the narrow, dirt path that bisected the open space. He stopped, looked up, and shaded his eyes with the back of his hand. Luke watched him as they buzzed by and saw the man's cap fly off from the tornado-like down draft caused by the rotors. The donkey bucked and lunged forward as the man retrieved his hat. A bundle of something fell from the animals back. The last thing Luke saw as he looked back was the man jumping around and shaking his fist after the metallic, hurricane-causing bird. Luke felt bad for the guy, but it was a funny site, and he couldn't suppress the slight smile that turned his lips.

Several minutes passed as rocky outcroppings, grass-filled open spaces, hillsides dotted with pine and oak, and a crystal clear, sky-blue tarn passed by. Some of the rocks and trees just a few feet below the wheels.

As they approached a small clearing surrounded by dense forest, Donnelly said, "That's it up ahead. Not much room, but we should be able to set down there."

Luke looked out and was glad to see the area was secluded. It would be a good drop-off and extraction point. He took the topo map out of his pocket and studied it. An animal trail to the right of the clearing was to be the starting point. The aircraft turned as it made its descent, and Luke saw that the trail was still there and well worn from recent use.

When the bird was on the ground, Donnelly turned in his seat and said, "This is it. We'll be back here as soon as we get the word that you're ready to return." He gave an informal salute. "Good luck."

Luke gabbed his rifle and said, "Thanks for the lift."

Donnelly said, "My pleasure," as Gomez waved.

Chuck gave his wide, shiny-white smile and said, "Don't forget us, now."

Both men hit the ground as the aircraft lifted. They crouched down and ran toward the tree line as dust and bits of loose grass swirled about.

10

JESÚS LÒPEZ MARTÌNEZ took a deep breath and let it out slowly just as his father had taught him to do. His finger moved slowly to the trigger, and when the last of his breath was out, just before breathing in again, he squeezed the trigger. The .22 popped as the cottontail made a death leap in the air before returning to earth, lifeless. At twelve years old, Jesús was already a better shot than his dad. A thin smile creased his lips as he stood to retrieve the rabbit. His dad will be proud. Another meal for only the cost of a bullet.

Jesús took a step and stopped. There was a strange buzzing sound coming from the ridge to the north. As the noise got louder, it became a slapping sound, and he knew it was a helicopter. He thought it might be Señor Quintana because he had the only helicopter around, but he never came from the north.

The boy didn't move. His eyes scanned the ridge as the buzzing got louder. When it crested the peak, the aircraft didn't look like anything he'd seen before. He ducked behind a rock to watch. It got louder and closer then set down in a clearing not more than fifty yards away.

He wondered if the Mexican Army was coming to try to get Señor Quintana. They'd tried before, but not around Gato Grande. Jesús knew it wasn't the Mexican Army as soon as the two men jumped out. They carried big guns and wore helmets and uniforms he'd never seen before. He ducked lower and peeked through a crack in the rock. As the helicopter lifted, the two men ran to the trees at the edge of the clearing and disappeared. Jesús watched until the aircraft vanished over the peak, heading north. The forest was silent except for the sound of a raven cawing in the distant trees. He listened but didn't hear any sound coming from the men.

When he was certain the men had left the area, Jesús rose and started to run two miles west to the one-room shack he shared with his father, leaving the rabbit behind. He was careful to stay low and hidden behind trees and rocks, staying to the valleys whenever possible, and stopping occasionally to listen.

Jesús was sweaty and out of breath when he reached home. He burst through the door with the story on his lips, but his father had not yet returned from town. He pulled a chair to the window and pressed the rifle to his chest as he surveyed the area around the shack, uncertain what he'd do if the men appeared.

Thankfully, the men didn't appear, and an hour later his father returned from the village leading their burro laden with jugs of water and sacks of beans, flour, salt, and vegetables. Jesús ran to him, shouting, "Papa. Papa. Papa. Guess what!"

"Whoa. Slow down, my son. Take a breath. What is it?"

"Two men. I saw two men from a helicopter."

"Probably Señor Quintana's men. Rumor has it he's coming soon."

"No, Papa. They weren't from Señor Quintana. Their dress wasn't like any I've seen before. They weren't Mexican. And the helicopter was different. They looked like the pictures I've seen of American soldiers."

"When did you see them? Where?

Jesús pointed to the east and said, "Maybe an hour and a half ago. Over the hill where I hunt."

The father's brow furrowed. He wondered if there might be a connection between the soldiers and Quintana's arrival. Miguel García Martinez didn't approve of all that Quintana did, but he had been given work at Palacio de Montaña many times when it was needed most. The money had provided food for him and his son, and the supplies used to build their home.

Miguel handed the burro's reins to Jesús, told him to unload the supplies and put the burro in the barn, then turned and started running back toward town. He looked over his shoulder as he ran and yelled, "Stay in the house. I'll be back soon."

11

ON A STREET corner in South Los Angeles, a skinny, disheveled, twenty-something man paced back and forth between a rusted and overflowing garbage can and the dim, flickering circle cast by the streetlight. His stringy black hair whipped his pock-marked face with each nervous jerk of his head. He felt in the pocket of his torn, dirty jeans to reassure himself the twenty crumpled one dollar bills he'd panhandled were still there. They were. It took Billy Fredrickson—Rat to those who knew him—most of the day to score the twenty. He hadn't had a fix since noon, and it was beginning to show. His movements were unsteady, his hands were shaky, his right eye twitched, and beads of sweat dotted his forehead. He wondered where his candy man was. The fucker had told him he'd be there at eight, and it had to be past that now.

Billy grew up in an affluent exurb of Omaha, Nebraska. His father was a dentist, and his mother taught school. His older brother was a successful artist living in Brooklyn, New York, and his younger sister was a Phi Beta Kappa at Penn State. Billy was the smartest, most talented of the three until a friend dared him to snort coke when he was fourteen. That's all it took. The coke habit grew until it was no longer enough. He graduated to heroin and has been an addict for the past seven years. He dropped out of high school in his junior year and just disappeared one night. Six months later, he was living on the streets of LA and panhandling for drug money whenever he was sober enough to stand.

The headlights of a dented 1967 Chevy Impala turned the corner a block down and swept the street in front of Billy. He stepped to the curb and out of the dull-yellow circle of light. The Chevy's bald tires slid as the driver braked. The passenger window inched down as the driver reached across and turned the handle.

"Rat. My man. What be goin' down?"

Billy reached back into his pocket and retrieved the hard-won cash. He thrust the wad of bills through the open window and said, "Here. You got it?"

The driver grabbed the money and said, "Hold your horses, man. Give me a sec." He unfolded each bill as Billy scanned the street first left, then right. Satisfied the money was all there, he handed Billy the small packet of white death he'd been waiting for.

Billy snatched the packet, put it in his pocket, and said, "Are you sure this shit's good?"

"Rat. Rat. You ask me the same damn thing every time. And I tell you the same damn thing every time. Yes, it's good. It's pure for Christ's sake. The Colima Cartel don't sell nothin' but the best. I know. I've tried it. And I get it directly from Quintana's mule hisself. So shut the fuck up and get outta here."

The tires screeched as the Impala pulled away from the curb and continued its nightly rounds of temporarily satisfying the never-ending craving of the downtrodden.

Billy limped across the street to the abandoned building where peaceful dreams awaited his return. He crawled through the broken window and slumped against a graffitied wall. The spoon, lighter, and borrowed syringe he'd used earlier in the day were still there. He put some of the powder in the spoon, cooked it to a dirty brown with the lighter, and filled the syringe. He pulled the belt tight around his thin, needle-tracked arm and inserted the needle. His whole body relaxed. The troubles of a moment before dissolved. A stuporous peace descended and all was right with the world.

Five minutes later, Billy "Rat" Fredrickson was dead. There was nobody there to miss him. His body was discovered four days later by a cop investigating a weird smell coming from the building.

12

LUKE LED THE way to the well-trodden animal trail, and they walked about half a mile before heading off the trail to a small, secluded clearing for a quick lunch. They had to keep their energy up if the mission was to be successful.

Luke leaned against a tree, and Chuck sat on a log. They'd packed enough MREs to last five days. To conserve space and keep their packs as light as possible, they'd removed all nonessential items, including flameless ration heaters, heating sleeves, water pouches, candy, gum, matches, and after-meal-mints. The cardboard packaging was left behind, and they'd each kept only one spork. The latter being a combination spoon-fork utensil.

Although it wasn't possible to eat a strictly vegan diet while on a mission, Luke packed only vegetarian meals: Vegetarian Taco Pasta, Elbow Macaroni and Tomato Sauce, Cheese Tortellini, and Spinach Mushrooms and Cream Sauce Fettuccini. Chuck on the other hand loaded up on all the meat he could get: Shredded BBQ Beef, Chicken Chunks, Beef Brisket, and Chicken Burrito Bowl.

Chuck said, "I thought I ate my last MRE back in Afghanistan."

"Yeah, me too. They're not that bad for a few meals. Hopefully, we'll be out of here long before our supply runs out. Hey, I thought you said you're a vegan. What's up with all the meat?"

"I may be a vegan back home, but not when I'm on

a mission. Haven't lost the taste for meat, and I'm still tempted by a very rare hunk of prime rib. In fact, I prefer it when they give me a knife and run the cow past the table."

Luke shook his head.

A twig snapped and they both froze, eyes glued in the direction of the sound. Luke silently unholstered his .45, and Chuck picked up his M-4. Time seemed to stand still as another twig snapped. This time the sound was noticeably closer. Their breathing was slow and easy.

A moment later a gray-brown patch appeared on the trail below. It moved slowly toward them. Heart rates elevated. The patch disappeared, and silence permeated the surrounding forest. Seconds passed. Then a set of five-point antlers appeared above the brush ten feet in front of Luke. They turned in Luke's direction, remained suspended above the bushes for a few moments, then quickly continued down the trail, rising and falling with each leap until they disappeared. The gentle breeze had prevented the buck mule deer from smelling the humans until it was practically on top of them.

Chuck took in a deep breath and said, "That got my blood flowing."

Luke took a drink from his camelback and policed the remains of his MRE. Chuck did the same, and they walked back to the trail. The path was rocky and soon ended at a rock outcropping. Luke surveyed the surrounding area, checked the topo map, and said, "It looks like heading uphill is our best bet. What do you think?"

"Yeah, I agree. It's too steep to go down, and we'll be more exposed."

Chuck took the lead, and they followed a narrow crevice to the top of the hill where trees and brush provided more cover. Luke pulled out his phone, did a compass reading, and they headed southwest in the general direction of Gato Grande.

The afternoon sun was hot even at that elevation. Although both men were in excellent shape, their clothing, boots, helmets, weapons, and heavy packs caused their foreheads to bead with sweat. They pressed on taking an occasional swig from their camel-backs. The going was slow, and they stopped to rest under the shade of a large oak. Quintana wasn't expected to arrive until the next afternoon, and they didn't have far to go. So there wasn't any need to hurry.

13

HEADS TURNED AS the doors to El Granero burst open, revealing a sweaty, out-of-breath Miguel Martìnez. His eyes swept the bar for the man he'd been talking with an hour earlier. The man wasn't there.

"Excuse me, gentlemen. Have you seen Diego Pérez? He was here an hour ago."

A man with stringy black hair, a skull tattoo on his arm, and menacing eyes looked up from the cards he was holding and said, "He left a few minutes ago. Why?"

"I need to talk to him. It's very important."

A gravelly voice at the end of the bar said, "Good luck."

A chorus of low laughs circulated the room.

Miguel spun around, pushed through the door, and stepped back onto the street. He shaded his eyes from the glaring sun and searched left and right for Pérez. Nothing. No one on the street. It was too hot. He turned to leave when he heard a vehicle behind him. He looked over his shoulder and saw a silver pickup turn the corner and head toward him. It was Pérez.

Miguel moved to the center of the road and frantically waved his arms. The truck stopped next to him, and the black-tinted window lowered, revealing a sober-faced Diego Pérez. With an expression that gave nothing, Pérez said, "Yes?"

In between gasps to catch his breath, Miguel said, "Diego … I'm sorry to bother you … but I thought you should know—"

"What is it?"

"—My son … He was out hunting—"

"Get to it, Miguel. I'm in a hurry."

Taking a deep breath, Miguel continued, "Forgive me, sir. My son was hunting when a strange thing happened. A helicopter landed about two miles form our house, and two men got out carrying guns. My son said they looked like American soldiers. The helicopter took off, and the men disappeared into the forest. I thought you should know."

"When did this happen?"

"About two hours ago."

"Is your son sure about what he saw?"

"Yes. I think so."

"You think so, or you know so?"

"I was not there, but my son is an honest boy. He wouldn't lie about something like that."

The truck sped off and left Miguel in a cloud of dust. He watched until the truck disappeared around a curve in the road, then slowly began the trek back home.

With the boss coming the next day, the news he'd just gotten was not good. Pérez pulled a cellphone from his pocket as he raced down the street. He punched in a number and held the phone to his ear.

A groggy voice answered with, "Yes?"

"Wake up, dammit. This is no time for a siesta. Get the drone ready. I'll be there in five minutes."

Pérez hung up, slammed the phone down on the seat, and punched the accelerator. The truck raced down the dirt road leading to Palacio de Montaña and flew past the gate in record time. It came to a sliding stop in front of the barn that doubled as an armory. Pérez jumped out and ran to the man standing at the door holding a DJI Inspire 2 drone and asked, "Is it charged?"

"Yes. Fully. What's going on?"

"We may have unwanted visitors. Set it down. I'm going to do an aerial survey. Get the men geared up in case we need to do boots on the ground reconnaissance."

The man set the drone on the ground and said, "Will do," as he ran toward the house.

The drone lifted and rose to five hundred feet. Pérez sat in his truck and flew the drone north while sweeping it left and right, covering two miles on either side of the ranch. His eyes were glued to the monitor for any sign of invaders.

When the drone was a mile north, Pérez had one of the men drive while he commanded the drone. After it had been up for twenty-five minutes, he flew it back to the truck to replace the battery with one that had a full charge. He'd thoroughly covered the area up to five miles from the ranch. Nothing. No soldiers anywhere.

With a fresh battery installed, the drone continued its flight north. It moved back and forth, providing a crystal-clear picture of every square inch of real estate. They covered another five miles before the second battery was drained and were well past the point where Miguel Martinez said his son saw the helicopter. Still nothing. That was a good thing. Pérez brought the drone back and had the driver take them back to the ranch. He was satisfied there was no imminent threat of attack.

14

LUKE LEANED BACK against the oak and watched a squirrel scamper up and down a tree, transporting acorns to some unseen hiding place. Chuck took advantage of the break to lie back on a bed of leaves and close his eyes. The rest conserved energy that might be needed later when sleep was not an option.

The squirrel was making its fourth trip up the tree when Luke thought he heard bees. He cocked his head in the direction of the sound. It was faint at first but seemed to be getting louder and closer. Realization dawned. It wasn't bees.

In a whisper, Luke said, "Chuck. Chuck. Do you hear that?"

"Hear what?"

"Listen. Do you hear that buzzing?"

Chuck focused his hearing, and after a moment said, "Yeah. I hear it."

"Does that sound familiar?"

"Yeah. It's a drone."

"Quintana's people may be reconning the area. Let's sit tight and see what happens."

"Roger that."

The buzzing ebbed and flowed. At times it disappeared completely only to return with greater intensity. Luke gripped his .45, ready to eliminate the threat if necessary. At one point, the drone hovered directly above them. Both men remained motionless, thankful for their camouflage uniforms.

The hum of the metal menace diminished then died. The sniper and spotter stayed frozen in place, breathing slow and steady, eyes scanning the visible horizon. Several minutes passed with no sound other than the murmuring breeze and cry of a distant hawk in search of a meal.

Luke said, "I think we're good."

"I don't believe they saw us?"

"No. The foliage is too thick, and we're almost indistinguishable from the leaves and twigs on the ground. Let's move out."

They shouldered the packs and picked up their rifles. Luke reviewed the topo map and did a compass reading before starting out. The going was slow at first, and the breeze died when they passed the downwind side of a high ridge. Another animal trail appeared and was heading in the direction they wanted to go. It made the hike much easier because the terrain leveled out and they didn't have to fight brush. But the heat was relentless.

Three more miles were behind them when animated laughter arose in the distance. It was high-pitched and seductive. Definitely female. But they didn't hear anyone talking. Luke moved closer to the boulder they were passing, and Chuck followed. The laughter grew louder when they reached the end of the boulder. Luke put up his hand to signal stop and said, "It sounds like it's coming from a little farther down the trail to our right."

Chuck nodded.

"Let's keep moving and see what we find."

They crept forward with slow, cautious steps. The laughter became more distinct, and voices could be heard. It was a woman, and a deep, resonant male voice responded to her. They were lively, happy sounds and didn't appear to be a threat. But because the couple was unknown to Luke and Chuck, extreme caution was needed.

A slight rise covered with grass and shrubs lay between the men and the couple. They hit the ground in a prone position and inched forward with their feet and elbows while holding their rifles. Luke was in the lead. He held and slowly released each branch that caught on his pack so it wouldn't hit Chuck or make noise that could give away their location. When they reached the top of the rise, Chuck moved up next to Luke, and they both peered through a tangle of grass and sticks to the small clearing ahead. Neither man was prepared for what he saw.

There was a blanket, a picnic basket, and an empty, tipped-over bottle of wine. But that isn't what caught the men's attention. Also on the blanket was a naked, prone man. And on top of the man was a beautiful, naked woman riding him like a horse. Her head was thrown back, and her breasts rose and fell with each undulation. Chuck felt his maleness become more firmly implanted to the ground. Neither man moved, although Luke averted his eyes after a moment. He wanted to continue watching but felt the couple deserved their privacy. Chuck, on the other hand, was all eyes forward.

The erotic scene finally erupted in a series of violent exhalations from the man and a very audible, "Oh … Dios," from the woman. The woman rolled off her partner, and they both lay gasping for breath as intermittent laughter bounced back and forth between them.

Chuck slowly turned his face to Luke as a smile

practically reached his ears and whispered, "Nature. Ain't it wonderful?"

Luke rolled his eyes.

It was another twenty minutes before the couple gathered themselves, dressed, picked up the remains of the picnic, and sauntered down the trail hand in hand; the woman's head resting on her man's shoulder.

Chuck's contact with the earth lessened, and he and Luke stood. Both were a bit distracted by what they'd just witnessed.

15

CASA VERDE IS a town in Southern Mexico named after the original settler of the area, Antonio Flores. Antonio was a nondescript, uneducated man who never married, had no children, spent as little time with people as possible, and grew maize his entire adult life. The only thing that made him stand out is the fact that he loved the color green, not just any green, but chartreuse green. A color halfway between yellow and green. Not the most soothing of colors. But according to legend, Antonio fell in love with it after seeing a bottle of Green Chartreuse liqueur as a small boy. No one knows where he saw the bottle because it was liqueur made in France by Carthusian Monks and was not known to exist in Mexico at the time. Due to his love of the color, he painted the interior and exterior of his house and all the furniture chartreuse green. And most of his clothes were that same color. In honor of their founder, several local markets now carry Green Chartreuse liqueur.

Not far from one of the liqueur-selling markets in the center of town was a small tavern called El Agujero. It was owned and operated by a middle-aged man, his wife, and their twelve-year-old son. For eight years they'd worked fourteen hours a day, seven days a week, serving drinks, tacos, and churros. The two-room apartment above was home.

El Agujero's customers were mostly men and women from the immediate area. It was a family gathering spot and place for people to grab a cold one after work. However, about six months ago Arturo Sánchez and his thugs began hanging out there in the afternoon when most people were working.

Sánchez was a young punk who wanted to be a big-time cartel boss. His operation was in its infancy, and he only grew and distributed marijuana. But he was trying to muscle his way into cocaine and heroin for the big bucks. Two weeks ago, he killed a Colima Cartel pilot and made off with several packages of cocaine worth over ten million dollars. That did not sit well with Quintana.

At 3:00 p.m. on a Tuesday, two weeks after the murder, a white Ford van pulled to the side of the street a block down from El Agujero. Three young men sat in front. They were unshaven, had long black hair and tattoos, and were very focused on the bar at the end of the street. They'd gotten word from Quintana that Sánchez and his gang would be there that afternoon. Hoping to impress the boss and move up in the organization, they were there on business.

The street was empty near the bar, and no one had gone in or come out since the men parked. Right on schedule at 3:15 p.m., an old blue Nissan stopped in front of the tavern. Six men got out. The first five were Sánchez's henchmen, and the last man out was Sánchez himself. They casually walked into El Agujero, not bothering to scan the street.

Quintana's men waited five minutes then exited the van and headed to the end of the street. They surveyed the surrounding area as they walked. Arrogance was apparent in the way they moved: heads cocked back, arms loose, and shoulders swaying left then right with each step. There were no weapons visible as they reached the entrance to the bar.

The three men entered El Agujero and stood in the open doorway silhouetted against the harsh afternoon sun. The room was dimly lit, and smoke curled up from the table where Sánchez and his men sat smoking and drinking. The owner looked up and stopped drying the glass he was holding. A concerned look etched on his face. His wife set down a plate of churros and turned to the open door. The twelve-year-old boy stopped sweeping and froze. The six men at the table turned. Their glasses poised in mid-salud.

One of the men at the door was holding an oblong, corrugated object in his right hand. He reached over with his left hand, removed a pin, and said, "Goodbye, assholes." The grenade bounced and rolled to the center of the room as the three men ran out the door. Sánchez and his men jumped up and started to scatter. The owner ran toward his son. The catatonic wife and mother stood motionless—a deer caught in the headlights.

Glass and debris blew from the windows and door as Quintana's men ducked behind a block wall next to the bar. Success. No more trouble from Sánchez. He was a menace that will not be missed. As for the collateral damage? To bad. But a small price to pay for fruitful revenge.

16

THE SNIPER TEAM pressed on in silence. After replaying the scene he'd just witnessed, Chuck said, "Whoa. That was a bonus to the mission."

"OK, horny man. Focus. We've got a job to do. Remember?"

"Yeah. Yeah. I know. But you gotta admit that was pretty cool."

Luke broke a smile.

The oppressive heat and humidity made for an arduous trek. An intermittent breeze brought little relief. Their packs seemed to get heavier with each step, but both men were in top physical condition. They adopted a consistent cadence that created a trance-like aura of calm while remaining hypervigilant of their surroundings. Flies buzzed, landed, ate, and buzzed some more around scat some animal had deposited next to the trail. Crows cawed, and an occasional butterfly danced over the scattered garden of wildflowers. A kettle of buzzards circled high in the air about a mile ahead.

Luke crested a low hill and came to a sudden halt. Chuck, still lost in the cadence, bumped into him. Luke raised his arm and pointed to the dell below. A momma cougar and two small cubs were tearing chunks of blood-red meat and guts from the body of a deer recently brought down. Momma and young stopped feasting, crouched low, and stared deep into the faces of the intruders. Not a muscle moved. The tension in the air was palpable. Neither Luke nor Chuck moved.

The stare down lasted a full ten seconds before momma made the wise decision to flee. Both she and the cubs raced into the brush with faces and paws smeared with blood and disappeared.

Luke said, "Looks like we're not alone."

"Yeah. I'm glad she decided to back down and not fight. I would have hated to take her out and leave her young to fend for themselves. They're so small the odds of survival without her are not good."

They moved on, keeping a watchful eye on rock outcroppings and other elevated areas because mountain lions typically attack from above. The cat didn't return, and their step regained a steady rhythm.

The temperature dropped a few degrees as the land fell away to the west, exposing them to the breeze working its way inland from the distant Pacific Ocean. It helped, but not much, because the terrain they were crossing began to slope upward at an ever-increasing angle.

Luke stopped to study the topo map. They were a couple of miles east of Gato Grande and about six miles from their primary position. Two to three hours should get them in place. A dirt road connecting Gato Grande to Ciudad de Cobra, a copper mining town farther up the mountain, was the only potential obstacle between where they were and where they wanted to be. Because both towns were small, the road didn't get much traffic. But Quintana's men had apparently been alerted to their presence, so caution was in order.

The road came into view about ten minutes later. Luke and Chuck assumed a prone position and raised their binoculars to scan the area. The forest grew right up to the edge of the two-lane, dirt roadway obstructing all of it but about fifty yards in either direction.

There were no people or cars on the road. Not a sound was heard other than the wind in the trees.

Chuck raised up on his knees and prepared to cross just as Luke pulled him back down. A late model Nissan pickup appeared out of the trees to the right and moved at a crawl toward them. Two men could be seen in the cab and two more were standing in the truck bed. They all held weapons as they searched the trees.

Luke and Chuck unholstered their .45s and remained motionless, hoping the tall grass provided sufficient cover.

The truck inched closer and passed without stopping. One of the men in the back appeared to look directly at Luke for a moment but then continued canvassing his side of the road. The truck was about to disappear into the trees to the left when brake lights came to life. Backup lights flashed on as the pickup retraced the ground it had just covered.

Luke and Chuck carefully moved their weapons forward.

The truck stopped about fifteen yards to the left of the snipers' position. The men in the back of the truck jumped out and headed toward the trees with their rifles held at the ready.

Luke slowly rotated his head to the left so he could observe what the men were doing. The man closest to Luke moved to within five yards of him but didn't spot him thanks to his camo suit and the tall grass.

The men walked a short distance into the trees, then shouldered their rifles and returned to the truck, laughing and talking. Luke picked up enough of the conversation to know that the men mistook a tree stump for a man.

The pickup continued down the road and disappeared.

Chuck said, "That was close."

"Too close. I thought we were going to have to start the fireworks sooner than planned."

They holstered their handguns, checked the road for other vehicles, and sprinted across the gravel and into the trees. The landscape leveled out and became easier to navigate as they neared their destination. About a mile and a half from their primary position, a faint buzz arose in the distance and grew louder as it approached.

Luke said, "It's coming back. Let's head to those bushes up ahead."

They ran to the brush and were hidden by the time the drone came into view. It passed directly overhead but kept on moving, zigzagging back and forth across the mountains. Luke and Chuck moved out when the aerial pest crested a far peak, and the buzzing ceased.

Chuck said, "Well, at least we know they've been tipped off to our presence."

"Maybe. Maybe not. It could be part of their regular routine in preparation for the boss's arrival."

"True."

"Either way, I'm sure our little visitor will be back. From here on in let's stick to the available cover as much as possible."

"Ten-four."

Twenty-five minutes later they arrived at their destination without further incident.

17

DAN COLBY WAS in his office reviewing updated intel on the Colima Cartel when a knock broke his concentration. "Come in."

Director Hewitt entered.

"Don. What's up?"

"A lot. I just received a message from our Colima source. We need to talk."

"Sure. Is there a problem?"

"I'm not sure. But the scope of Operation Wolf Hunt has definitely changed."

"How so?"

"Apparently, Francisco Aguilar and Alejandro Bardales are meeting with Quintana at Palacio de Montaña day after tomorrow."

"Whoa!"

"Yeah, whoa! Aguilar's Chiapas Cartel and Bardales's Hidalgo Cartel are the two bigest drug operations in Mexico, after Quintana. Some say they're more violent and have caused more death and suffering than Quintana. Either way, they're bad characters. Our Operation Wolf Hunt has the potential to make an even greater impact than we'd planned."

Colby hit some keys on his computer and pulled up recent photos of the two drug lords.

Hewitt continued. "Do you think our boys can handle this?"

"Luke is the best sniper the SEALs have ever produced, and although Chuck is acting as spotter, his sniper skills are right up there with Luke's. That's why they were assigned together. They're a deadly team. Chuck is carrying a MK 15, so he can be effective long distance."

"Of course, security at the ranch is going to be much tighter with three of them there. That's going to make the mission significantly more dangerous."

Colby looked at the time on his computer and said, "The boys should be at their primary location soon. They're gonna contact me when they get there. I'll pull up photos of Aguilar's and Bardales's security teams and get them to Luke and Chuck ASAP. They'll have an extra day to prepare since the guests aren't arriving until day after tomorrow."

As Hewitt walked to the door, he said, "I'll let you know if I get any more from our source. I want to know what the boys have to say. Give me a call when you hear."

"Will do."

Colby opened the DATACOM file on his computer and was copying photos of the security teams and any other information on the cartels he thought might be useful when his satellite phone vibrated. It was Luke.

"Luke. Are you in place?"

"Yeah. We just arrived. It was a little slow going, but we made it. Quintana's people may have gotten word that we're here. We were buzzed twice by a drone and saw some of Quintana's men on the road out of Gato Grande. They were armed and searching—maybe for us."

"Well get ready because I just got word from Hewitt that things may get a bit more complicated down there"

"Great. How so?"

"Quintana is expecting guests."

"Do we know who?"

"We do. Have you heard of Francisco Aguilar, also known as "El Tigre," and Alejandro Bardales, better known as "Mal Culo?""

"Yeah. They both rank right up there with Quintana on the evil scale. But I thought they hated one another. They've been fighting for years."

"They have been. But, word has it, they want to end the intercartel competition and combine their expertise and resources to become more efficient, more dominant, and even wealthier."

"When are they supposed to arrive?"

"Quintana should get there tomorrow with the guests arriving the next day. That gives you an extra day to prepare."

"What's their ETA?"

"Don't know that, but I'm sure you'll hear them coming."

"Do we know how many security personnel they're bringing?"

"Not specifically. But you can count on a bunch. Both Aguilar and Bardales typically travel with six of their best men. So you can expect at least a dozen, and they'll be arriving by helicopter."

"Three helos, a drone, and at least nineteen guards. That should make for a challenging escape and evasion."

"It won't be easy, but we'll download real time satellite surveillance to your phones. That will help even out the odds a bit. I have faith in you guys."

"Thanks. We're gonna need it."

"Aguilar heads the Chiapas Cartel and Bardales leads the Hidalgo Cartel. I'm compiling a file with photos of the bosses and their security details along with the most current intel on their operations. I'll have it to you within the hour. Is your primary position gonna work?"

"We just got here, but it looks good so far. We're about a mile and a half from the target with plenty of cover and several escape options. We'll check out the other positions we discussed, but the primary has a good view of the back of the house, cabana, and pool area."

"Great. Luke, this is one hell of an opportunity to put a big dent and a little fear in the world of drug lords. Do you think it's possible to take out all three?"

"Possible, but not probable. With Chuck shooting, too, we might get a couple, but to chamber another round and get it off before the third guy takes cover is unlikely."

"Understand. Just give it your best, as I'm sure you will. Quintana is the primary target. Anything more is a bonus."

"Got it."

The call ended.

Luke leaned back against a boulder and looked at Chuck, who had his binoculars pressed to his eyes, surveilling the ranch and surrounding area, and said, "Well, big guy, you ready to do some shooting?"

"Say what?"

"Are you ready to do some shooting?"

"Sure. What's up?"

"Just got word that our friendly wolf is gonna have company. Not just any company, but Francisco Aguilar and Alejandro Bardales."

"No shit? When?"

"Day after tomorrow. Apparently, the big three are going to try to make nice and work together."

"Wow! And we're supposed to take out all three?"

"If we can. Quintana remains the primary target, but Colby'd like to have the others eliminated, if possible. I told him it's possible, but not probable."

"I'm glad I got off some rounds back in Virginia. It's been a while since I was the shooter."

"I know you. You'll do great."

"Let's hope."

"What's going on at the ranch?"

"Not much. The drone came back while you were on the horn. It looks pretty quiet for now, but I'm sure things will pick up when the boss arrives tomorrow."

"I'm going to choke down another MRE and then check out more of the area before we lose the light."

"Sounds good. Well, maybe not *good*, but I don't see any restaurants close by."

18

DIEGO PEREZ SAT in his office cleaning the drone's camera lens and charging the batteries. Everything had to be ready for the boss's arrival the next morning. He'd already inspected the armory to ensure that all weapons were clean, loaded, in their proper place, and that ammunition for each was readily available. A thorough check of the munitions, vehicles, house, outbuildings, and surrounding area was always performed just prior to Quintana's appearance at the ranch. Extraordinary preparation was called for given the unprecedented nature of this visit. Never had the three most powerful Mexican drug lords met face-to-face. It was a historic event that could radically change the way drugs are manufactured, transported, and distributed. Narcos would feel the effects worldwide if the meeting were successful.

Perez called out to the man passing his office. "Hey, Luis."

"Yes?"

"How's it going with the vehicles?"

"Good. I've completed maintenance, washed, and gassed up your truck and both vans. I'm on my way to do the Humvee now."

"Let me know when you're finished. I have a list of supplies for you to pick up in town."

Luis said, "OK," and walked on.

Rosa Campo was a large woman, wide, not tall. She had short, curly black hair, a round face, and sausage-like fingers that exemplified her love for the fruits of her labor. She was Quintana's cook and lived in one of the cottages at the ranch. She'd been married to a physically abusive man until El Lobo put an end to her suffering. Her husband was never seen again, and she has been devoted to her savior ever since. A limp and a scar traversing the right side of her face from her ear to her chin served as memorials to her husband's alcoholic rages.

This morning, she and her assistant, Leticia, were busy cleaning the kitchen, restocking the pantry and walk-in cooler with the groceries that had been dropped off earlier, and marinating the venison to be served at lunch the next day. It was wearisome work, especially for legs that continuously argued with Rosa about her weight.

Javier Abarca sat in the gun turret on top of the house, cleaning the .50 caliber machine gun and scanning the surrounding meadow and forest for any unwanted company. The shoulder-fired Stinger missile launcher was loaded and ready for action. Six backup missiles lay nearby for quick access. Abarca was forty. He'd served ten years with the Mexican Army before being unceremoniously drummed out after almost killing one of the men in his unit for making a disparaging comment about his mother. He spent the next ten years as a mercenary in the Middle East fighting for whichever cause paid the most. Quintana has been his cause for the past two years.

Miguel Guzmán and Raúl Herrera, both in their early sixties, have known Quintana since he was a small boy. They'd worked with his father in a small machine shop for sixteen years until the owner died and the shop closed. The men fell on hard times and survived doing odd jobs until Quintana rose to the top of the cartel and hired them to manage the grounds of his ranch. Today, Miguel was skimming the pool and adding chemicals while Raúl tended to the landscaping. Their appreciation for having work resulted in the meticulously maintained premises.

Maria Sandoval and Yolanda Magro were mother and daughter. Maria's husband ran off with another woman when Yolanda was a baby, and she took in laundry to provide food for her child. Yolanda married when she was sixteen to a kind, handsome young man she'd known since they'd learned to walk. She lost him shortly after the wedding when his motorcycle was struck by a car driven by the local drunk. When Quintana heard about the tragedy, he brought them to the ranch as housekeepers for the main house and guest quarters. They've kept the place spotless for seven years.

Four of the guards sat in the cabana playing malilla with a traditional 40-card deck, smoking unfiltered Delicados cigarettes, and drinking beer before the boss arrived, and they had to be alert and sober. They'd completed their rounds of the property and checked their weapons. It was time for a little R&R before the long days and nights of surveillance kicked in. Javier would let them know if there was a problem.

Luis Fuentes topped off gas in the Humvee, picked up the supply list from Perez, and bounced down the road toward Gato Grande in his rusted 1978 BMW. It barely ran, but hey, it was a BMW after all.

Things were shaping up for the historic meeting.

19

LUKE'S EYES SHOT open revealing a night sky punctuated by stars and the reflected sunlight of planets. He didn't move. Chuck was three feet to his right, in the arms of Morpheus, and driving pigs to market. The buzzing was distant at first but getting louder. Luke whispered, "Chuck. Chuck. Stop snoring and wake up."

Chuck didn't budge.

Luke was about to add more volume to his plea when the sound retreated, and his mental acuity sharpened on the cool night air. It wasn't a drone, only an eager mosquito in search of a meal. He closed his eyes and tried to go back to sleep, but the first soft light of a new day was peeking over the eastern horizon. He was awake.

Chuck continued driving pigs, as Luke rolled over, grabbed his binoculars, and combed the valley below. The house was dark. A lookout was posted at each corner of the property, rifle in hand, and a fifth man, stationed in the turret on top of the house, scanned the meadow and tree line with binoculars. It wouldn't be long before Quintana arrived.

Chuck awoke with a start. Apparently, Morpheus had dropped him.

Luke gave a quiet laugh and said, "Morning, sunshine. Did you get the pigs to market?"

Chuck stretched, yawned, and said, "What?"

"Nothing."

"What are you doing?"

"Just checking things out down below."

"Anything yet?"

"No. The house is still dark, but security is keeping a sharp eye on the place. The big man will be here soon."

Chuck picked up his collapsible shovel and headed into the ravine behind them to drop the kids off at the pool, although there was no pool, thus the shovel. Luke leaned back against a rock and tore open a Cheese Tortellini MRE for breakfast. Chuck returned refreshed and opened a packet of Chicken Chunks for his meal.

After breakfast, they donned their ghillie suits and stuck tall grass in the foliage ring of their boonie hats. The scattered boulders and tall grass provided excellent cover. They were virtually invisible as they crawled to a forward position that afforded an unobstructed view of the ranch and surrounding grassland. Luke trained his binoculars on the house and adjacent buildings while Chuck covered the open space. Thanks to the elevation and a steady breeze out of the west, the temperature inside the ghillie suits was bearable. At lower elevation and without the breeze, the heat would be insufferable.

The goon in the turret spent the morning inspecting the property while others continued preparing for the arrival of the boss and his guests. The pesky drone took off and landed numerous times throughout the morning, each time it patrolled the forest up to a mile out from the house. It appeared the thugs didn't believe it was necessary to patrol farther out. That was a good thing for Luke and Chuck since they were approximately a mile and a half away.

Luke checked the time, saw it was 11:46 a.m., and said, "Are you hungry? This might be a good time to eat since The Wolf could check in at any time."

"Yeah. Let's do it."

They'd just started to move back when Luke raised his hand, palm out. Chuck heard it too and stopped. The familiar *whop whop whop* of helicopter blades could be heard far to the south. The aircraft appeared as a small dot on the horizon a few seconds later.

Chuck said, "So much for lunch."

"He's early. Let's stay on him awhile. We can alternate eating later."

The bird landed on the helipad adjacent to the house. The engine shut down, and the blades slowed as two men got out, followed by a woman. The three made their way toward the front of the house. One of the men was security. The other was the target. The woman was Quintana's mistress. The pilot got out and followed close behind. Both the pilot and the man walking with Quintana shouldered rifles.

At five feet six and one hundred-thirty pounds, Quintana looked like a kid compared to the hulk walking next to him. The guy appeared to be six feet seven and three hundred pounds. Luke wondered how such a diminutive man was able to command such power. Perhaps evil trumps size.

The woman was tall and elegant. Her long black hair caressed the small of her back as she walked. The sway of her hips suggested runway model. She was at least four inches taller than her paramour. She was beautiful, her man not so much. The contrast bespoke the lure of power and wealth.

The four new arrivals disappeared into the house while the outside security remained vigilant. The boss and his girlfriend reappeared mid-afternoon and ensconced themselves on padded recliners next to the pool. He wore a candy-red Speedo, and she wore a black thong—at least it looked like a thong, but who knows, given the color of her hair.

Two of the outside security details positioned themselves at each end of the pool while one of the inside men kept the margaritas flowing. The gold digger rubbed lotion on the hairy, Speedo-clad body next to her, and her illicit mate returned the favor—not missing an inch of skin, and dallying in certain areas much longer than needed to apply a sufficient coat of sunscreen.

Luke and Chuck took it all in from their distant perch. Given their current situation, both thought that the margaritas looked the best. Although, the lotion party was a strong second.

Rose colored clouds to the west heralded the end of Quintana's first day back at the ranch. He and his lover returned to the house as night enfolded the scene. The men to the north shed their ghillie suits and boonie hats, swallowed another MRE, and turned in. The next day promised to be much more exciting.

20

THE PIVOTAL DAY dawned cool and dry with a clear sky and no wind, excellent conditions for the task at hand. Luke had just finished his breakfast MRE when his satellite phone vibrated. It was Colby.

"Colby, what's up?"

"I received an email from our Colima contact a few minutes ago. He confirmed the meeting is on and said both Aguilar and Bardales should arrive in about an hour with their security teams. They'll be coming by helicopter and leaving sometime in the afternoon. The window of opportunity is narrow, so if you get a good shot, take it and get the hell out of there. I'll be monitoring you by satellite feed."

"I assume we're still looking at six security personnel per team?"

"That's my understanding."

"OK. Thanks for the update. We'll get things policed, pack up, and be in position in a few minutes. Let us know if anything changes."

"Will do. Be careful, Luke. These are very dangerous men."

"Roger that."

Luke disconnected the call and gave Chuck the news. They put on their ghillie suits, collected their gear, and made ready for a speedy exit. They had reviewed the escape routes many times, so there would be no hesitation once the target—hopefully, targets—was down.

Luke grabbed his rifle and binoculars and crawled

to the FFP: final firing position. He double checked to make sure the bullet path he'd cleared was still free of grass or anything else that the bullet could cause to move. It was. The activity below indicated the guests would be there soon.

Chuck got his rifle and field glasses, moved into position next to Luke, and cleared a blade of grass that had bent down into the bullet path since he'd last cleared it. He joined Luke in surveilling the target area and said, "You ready?"

"As ready as I'll ever be. You?"

"Yeah. A little nervous."

"A little nervous is good. There'd be something wrong if you weren't. It keeps you sharp"

"I'm glad we got all that practice in back at Langley."

"Me too."

Chuck began calling out stats for the shot. "Temperature is sixty-eight degrees here. Should be about sixty-nine near the pool. No wind. Relative humidity is fifty-two percent. Barometric pressure is 29.52 inches. Our altitude is 2,600 feet, and we're 250 feet above the target area. We're 2,602 yards from the edge of the pool nearest the house, and the back of the house is another twelve yards beyond that."

"Thanks, man."

Chuck resumed scanning the house and adjacent buildings.

The hum of the drone was constant as it circled the meadow and nearby trees, never going farther out than a mile from the house. The idiots didn't realize what awaited them a half mile beyond their search perimeter.

Forty-five minutes after Colby's call, the distinctive slap of helicopter blades arose to the south and grew in intensity as the chopper neared the ranch. It circled the property, evaluating the situation on the ground, and landed on the grass next to the helipad. The door opened, and two burly thugs stepped out wearing black pants, black T-shirts, and shouldering automatic weapons. They crouched low to avoid the rotor downwash of the still-rotating blades. Aguilar was next, followed by three more identically dressed and armed goons. Aguilar wore tan slacks and an untucked Hawaiian shirt; his salt and pepper hair danced wildly around his face. They moved away from the aircraft and waited for the pilot to shut down the engine. The pilot emerged completing the gang of sextuplets. He joined the others as they made their way to Quintana and his men, who were waiting on the veranda.

Quintana held out his arms, palms up, as the men approached, and said, "Welcome, my friend. Welcome to Palacio de Montaña."

"Thank you, Carlos. It's good to finally meet."

The security teams locked eyes and remained hypervigilant. Neither side wanting to show any weakness.

The Wolf and The Tiger moved into the house, followed by four other men, two from each security team. The remaining eight men spread out to keep an eye on the outside. Luke and Chuck followed their every move through glasses that made it seem as though they were walking with them.

Ten minutes later, the distant drone of another helicopter could be heard approaching from the south. All heads on the ground turned to face the sound. Quintana and Aguilar stepped out onto the porch along with the four men who'd followed them in.

The aircraft flew straight in and set down next to

Aguilar's chopper. Bardales and his men followed the same routine used by Aguilar and his people for exiting the helicopter, and their dress was identical: black pants, black T-shirts, and shouldering automatic weapons. They must have coordinated before taking off.

They strode across the lawn to where Quintana and Aguilar waited. Arrogance was evident in the way Bardales moved: erect, shoulders swaying, head cocked to the side.

The three drug barons exchanged cursory hugs while their security teams stood back and warily scrutinized one another. The exchange was brief and to the point. Quintana stepped aside and motioned his guests inside. He followed them trailed by two members of each security detail. The twelve men assigned to exterior duty split up and walked the property, including all outbuildings. They presented a formidable show of force that most would be reticent to approach. But the formidability diminished when they could be dealt with from afar without direct contact.

The initial greeting took place on the porch on the south side of the house and out of the snipers' view. They could have taken out Aguilar or Bardales as the men approached the house, but Quintana was the primary target, and he remained hidden by the porch roof. They'd have to remain vigilant and wait for the perfect shot.

21

LUKE AND CHUCK stayed alert to the activity below. An hour passed, then two, then three with no sign of Quintana or his guests. The security details continued their patrol of the area around the house while the eyes in the turret did a steady 360-degree sweep of the tree line. The drone made its rounds every thirty minutes like clockwork.

Luke said, "Go take a break. You'll be more effective when the action starts. I'll let you know if anything changes."

"I'll be right behind you. Let's switch every fifteen minutes."

"Sounds good."

Chuck crawled back out of the FFP and into the ravine that served as base camp. He removed his boonie hat to let his head breathe, took a drink of water, and ate an energy bar. It felt good to relax the concentration.

Luke continued to monitor the ranch for any sign of the three narcos. It was tedious work, but necessary to ensure not missing an opportunity to engage the target. You might only get one chance at a shot, and it may only last a few seconds. Luke and Chuck had waited and watched a cave entrance for six days before taking out their last terrorist target in Afghanistan.

Luke lowered his binoculars for a moment to rest his eyes—and there it was. Out of the corner of his eye, he saw the black, red, and yellow bands of the thin ophidian he'd hoped to avoid: a coral snake. It was about fifteen inches long, and the deadliest snake in Mexico. He froze. The serpent slowly slithered its way through the tall grass a mere eighteen inches in front of his nose. One bite had the potential to kill a person. Luke had a snakebite kit, but that would only delay death for a short time until he could get medical attention. Given his current location, the odds of getting help before his respiration was compromised were not good. Time seemed to stand still. Seconds seemed like minutes, and minutes seemed like hours.

The colorful ribbon of death finally slid out of Luke's peripheral vison and vanished around a large boulder. He took a deep breath, and his breathing returned to normal. He raised the glasses hoping he hadn't missed an opportunity below. Nothing had changed. The security goons continued their robotic walk, following the same course they were on the last time he looked.

Chuck crawled back into position after his break and said, "Anything shakin'?"

"Nothing so far. However, I was interrupted for a couple of minutes while a coral snake cruised by to check me out."

"No shit?"

"Yeah. It was right in front of my face. I could have reached out and grabbed it."

Whoa! Those things can be deadly. Do you think it's gone?"

"It slithered around the boulder to my left and disappeared, so I think we're good. But be alert."

Luke lowered his binoculars and started to crawl to the ravine for a break while Chuck picked up the surveillance. He had only moved back a few feet, when Chuck said, "We've got movement."

Luke crawled back into position and scoped out the scene below.

"What'd you see?"

"One of the maids came out and put what looks like a cigar humidor on the table in the cabana."

"I see it."

"She went back inside, but some of the security are repositioning closer to the pool. Something's up."

"They probably reached a working agreement and are adjourning to the pool to celebrate."

"And we've got a clear view into the cabana."

"Things are about to get interesting."

Three of the goons stationed themselves at the far side of the pool opposite the cabana. Three others took up positions near the cabana.

Maria Sandoval came out carrying a large platter of fresh fruit topped with Tajin seasoning and placed it on the table. The spicey fruit was one of Quintana's favorite snacks. Her daughter, Yolanda, followed close behind with two large bowls. One was filled with salty corn chips called Takis that were abundant at every Quintana gathering, and the other overflowed with dried salted plums called saladitos that were another Quintana favorite. Maria reappeared and set a place mat, small plate, and colorfully decorated ashtray on the table in front of each chair. Yolanda returned and placed a finger bowl and large linen napkin next to each place mat because the red dye in the Takis was nearly impossible to get off.

A butterfly flitted among the bougainvillea blossoms that snaked up the cabana support columns and encased the roof in a burst of red while guards stood silent, discretely shifting weight from one foot to another. The drone circumnavigated the nearby woods while "Turretman" glassed the perimeter. The .50 cal was locked and loaded, and the rocket launcher stood at the ready.

22

CHUCK SET DOWN his rifle to check current conditions. He called them out as each was confirmed. "Temperature is now seventy degrees here. Should be about seventy-one at the cabana. Still no wind. Relative humidity is steady at fifty-two percent. Barometric pressure is 29.50 inches. Our altitude is 2,600 feet, and we're 250 feet above the target area. We're 2,602 yards from the edge of the pool nearest the house, the back of the house is another twelve yards beyond that, and the nearest side of the cabana is 2,606 yards."

"You the man."

"I know."

Chuck picked up his rifle and continued to scope out the back of the hacienda. A bee landed on the muzzle of his gun and stared down the barrel at him. It rubbed its back legs together, spread its wings, and rose. The ghillie suit was hot, especially with no breeze, and sweat beaded down his temples from the brim of his boonie hat. He whispered, "Come on you nefarious narcos. Show yourselves."

Luke inserted the tube of his hydration pack into his mouth and took a couple of swallows. The liquid was no longer cool but felt good to his parched throat. His Vegetarian Taco Pasta breakfast had worn off an hour ago, but lunch would have to wait as the target could present himself at any moment.

Another ten minutes passed before a diminutive man with a shaved head and a soul patch stepped out of the house and walked to the cabana. It was Quintana. His ever-present five-o'clock shadow looked like it had been drawn on with a black marker.

Aguilar was next, followed by Bardales. Aguilar was tall, angular, well-muscled, with straight black hair tied back in a ponytail. A scar split his face from the left ear to the corner of his mouth. Bardales was average height, soft, gray haired, with a paunch that preceded him wherever he went. Four black teardrops were etched at the corner of his left eye. The men took their seats in the cabana. Quintana sat with his back to the snipers. Aguilar sat to his left, and Bardales took the chair to his right.

Chuck said, "The odds of getting all three are not good," when Aguilar, not wanting to be in the sun, stood and moved to the chair directly across from Quintana.

"Look at that, will ya? Could this be the day for a twofer?"

"Could be. If anyone can do it, I'd put my money on you, my friend."

"I heard of one time when it was done. Unfortunately, the second guy was an innocent bystander."

"Well there ain't no innocent bystanders in this bunch. Any secondary hit would be a positive."

Just then, Quintana stood up, pulled his cell phone out of his pocket, and went into the house.

A whispered "Shit" escaped Luke.

"He'll be back."

"Hopefully, he'll take the same seat."

Yolanda appeared with three ice-cold Coronas and set one on each place mat before returning to the house. Aguilar and Bardales kept conversation to a minimum while they sipped beer and helped themselves to the spicey snacks. Aguilar swatted at a fly that had a taste for saladitos. Bardales let out a loud burp and threw a thin smile at Aguilar.

Quintana stepped onto the patio and ended the call. He put the phone back in his pocket and returned to the same seat he'd occupied earlier. He looked back and forth between his guests, waved his hands high above his head, and then slammed his fists on the table. The other men clapped and laughed.

Quintana passed the cigar humidor around the table. Each man picked out a Churchill, lit it, sat back in his chair, and blew out a gust of smoke that drifted lazily above their heads before dispersing. They seemed relaxed.

Luke sent a quick text to Colby to let him know they were about to engage. Colby confirmed that he had activated the satellite feed and was watching them in real-time.

Luke glanced at Chuck and said, "How ya lookin'?"

"Good. Bardales should be easy. He doesn't move much, and his head's the size of a watermelon. I've got a clear shot of the left side of his head and body with no obstructions."

"I've got Quintana and Aguilar lined up. Let's do it."

"Ready here."

"I'll do a three count. Let's get the shots off together, if possible."

"Roger that."

"One." Deep breath, exhale. "Two." Deep breath, exhale. "Hold it. The girl is back with more beer."

"Standing down."

Yolanda set the beers down and picked up the empties along with a bowl that had been filled with Takis, and then walked back into the house.

Luke said, "The girl's going to refill the bowl she took and come back out. Let's give her a minute. I don't want this to go down with her nearby. It's going to be ugly enough for her as it is without her seeing it go down."

"Agreed."

The drone made a pass around the edge of the meadow and returned to the barn. The guy in the turret seemed to have his binoculars trained at the snipers' location. Neither Luke nor Chuck moved. After an interminable few seconds, he continued to pan the area.

Yolanda returned with the bowl overflowing with Takis, set it down in the middle of the table, did a slight curtsy in Quintana's direction, and disappeared through the door. The men simultaneously reached for the bowl.

Once the men settled back in their chairs, Luke said, "Ready to go again?"

"Ready."

"OK. Here goes. One ... Two ... Three." Both triggers were pulled in unison. Luke and Chuck continued to monitor the action through their scopes.

In less than two seconds, three heads exploded. Bardales painted the cabana support post nearest him a bright red as he flew out of his seat and landed on the tile floor of the cabana. A round passed through the back of Quintana's head and through Aguilar's left eye before mottled gray matter from Quintana's brain decorated Aguilar's face. Aguilar flew over backward and cracked his head on the tile. Not that it made any difference at that point. Quintana did a face plant—at least what was left of it—in a plate of Tajin-flavored fruit: a fitting end since it was one of his favorite snacks.

The bullets traveled at Mach 3 and broke the sound

barrier, causing a boom to echo through the hills. The confused security goons looked in every direction, trying to locate the threat. One of them spotted a vapor trail coming from the hills to the north and yelled to the others, "Over there." He waved and pointed to the spot where he'd seen the now-dissipated vapor trail.

The drone rose and flew at top speed to the north. The .50 cal was swiveled north, and the turret guard scoured the hills, looking for any sign of the intruders. In an attempt to kill or flush out the threat, he set the binoculars down, got behind the .50 cal, pulled the charging handle back, released it, and began to pepper the forest from the edge of the meadow to the top of the ridge with 600 rounds a minute. The devastation was mind-blowing. Shattered branches fell from trees, dirt and rock leaped from the ground in a hundred locations at once, and birds rose in the air—not all of them successfully. God knows how many animals, both large and small, lay dead or dying.

After confirming the kills, Luke and Chuck backed out of their FFP and into the ravine. They were well outside the .50 cal's effective range, but well within its maximum range. The area they were in was sprayed with rounds every few seconds, bringing life to inanimate objects. They grabbed their gear and were heading down the ravine when the now-familiar hum of the drone rose above the ridge. Luke turned to face the menace and hit the ground. Chuck did the same. The camera moved from side to side as it checked the area. The ghillie suits provided cover, and not spotting anything out of the ordinary, the drone turned west and disappeared over the trees.

The snipers stood, crouched low, and ran northeast through a ravine that provided the best escape route. It zigged and zagged through the rocks under a protective cover of pine trees. They hadn't gone fifty yards when the whir of a helicopter approached from behind. Fortunately, they were in a clump of trees and sheltered by a canopy of pine branches. The bird flew directly above them and continued heading north.

A text message arrived from Colby. *Watching you from the heavens. Drone far west. 2 choppers on ground. The other 1.2 clicks ahead. 10 men heading your way.*

Luke said, "Let's go. We've got company on the way."

"Surprise. Surprise."

Trees continued to provide cover for another 100 yards before they came to a clearing with no way around. It would have to be crossed.

Colby texted. *2nd bird up. No one close.*

Luke said, "Let's go. We're clear."

The men ran across the open space keeping an eye to the sky. They made it to an area of thick brush.

Colby texted. *Bird heading your way.*

The distant sound of rotor blades could be heard as Luke read the text. Both men found a bush and dove under it. The helicopter came to within forty yards of their location, hovered, and did a three-sixty. Two men could be seen at the open door. They each held an AK-47 as they scanned the ground. Not seeing a threat, the chopper flew on.

Luke and Chuck jumped up and ran through the brush. The ravine ended at a steep rock face where an animal trail curved to the left and disappeared farther down the mountain. It would take them closer to Gato Grande, but the terrain was more even, allowing them to move faster. They hit the trail running, sliding in the loose dirt when the path steepened. Halfway down, they got another text from Colby. *Bird coming back.*

They ran as fast as the terrain would allow, hoping to make the trees. No such luck. The chopper crested the ridge and came into view when they were in the open. Bullets tore up the ground around them, but thanks to the movement of the helicopter, they weren't hit.

Luke wedged himself into a crack in the nearby rocks and pulled Chuck in with him. There was barely enough room for the two of them, and Chuck was still partially exposed. The bird hovered thirty yards out as rounds exploded the rock, covering both men with dust and shards of stone. Chuck ripped the grenade launcher from his shoulder and got a round off as the aircraft steadied. The earth-shattering explosion brightened the daylight and rattled the ground as two flaming bodies fell on the rocks, and fragments of helicopter littered the ground.

Luke said, "Thanks, man. Well done," as he and Chuck got back on the trail and continued downhill.

Colby texted. *Holly shit! That was close. Well done, Chuck. Chopper and drone coming. Men on ground 1-mile SE.*

They ran on the trail until it entered dense brush that was too thick to navigate. They turned north again and entered an area thick with trees and scattered boulders. The sound of the helicopter grew louder as it closed in on them.

Luke said, "We've got to make a stand here. They know where we are and won't go away without a fight. The area ahead is more open, so taking them on here is our best option."

"Roger that."

"There's a group of rocks ahead that should give us cover on three sides and partial cover from above.

They'll have to take us head on. What do you think?"

"Yeah. I don't see a better option. Let's do it."

Chuck set his rifle against the rocks and shouldered the grenade launcher. Luke took up a position next to Chuck and readied his rifle. The buzz of the still-distant helicopter was overshadowed by the hum of the drone as it wended its way through the trees, panning left and right in search of its prey.

Luke focused his attention in the direction of the oncoming threat. It suddenly broke through the trees to his right, twenty feet off the ground, and turning slow three-sixties. Luke got it in the cross hairs of his sight and waited until it cleared the final tree branch before becoming completely exposed. It hadn't yet spotted them when Luke squeezed the trigger and turned the four-bladed beast into a spray of scrap parts.

Luke said, "Bingo!"

"Oh, yeah. That'll keep the drone pilot guessing."

The celebratory moment was cut short when the helicopter came into view above the trees in front of them. Like the drone, it was doing three-sixties while the rifle-wielding thugs searched the ground for the culprit or culprits who'd snuffed out their boss.

Chucked dropped into position with the chopper in his sight when the first shots rang out. They were wild and ricocheted off the rocks protecting the snipers. Chuck got off a shot before the helicopter steadied enough for the goons to get accurate. The explosion echoed through the forest and bounced off the rock-faced peaks as the bird pitched nose down and disintegrated into a pile of flaming metal.

Luke let out a "Hooyah" and high-fived Chuck as Colby's text arrived. *Awesome, guys! That was awesome.*

Now get the hell out of there. The ground goons are moving in about three-quarters of a mile to your tail.

They shed their heavy, hot ghillie suits so they could travel faster and moved out.

23

GABRIELA GONZÁLEZ WAS beautiful, twenty-three, and living alone on a small farm a mile east of Gato Grande. She was born on the farm, raised there, and stayed on after her parents contracted influenza and died when she was eighteen. She was intelligent, strong, and a hard worker. The farm kept her busy and provided the food to sustain her with enough left over to sell at the market in town. The cash covered her few needs.

Gabriela's hate for Quintana and his men was born out of an incident that occurred on her nineteenth birthday. She was walking home after spending the day in town with her friend, Josefina. She'd just left the main street in town and turned down the dirt road that led to her farm when she heard the drunken laughter of men. The voices were familiar to her from the many times she'd been catcalled while shopping in town. They were rude, disgusting men—pigs, really. However, she considered the latter reference an insult to the even-toed ungulates that serve as both friend and food. She picked up her pace while continuing to check the road behind her. The men saw her and began to run in her direction. Gabriela started to run, hoping to get to her house before the men caught up to her. She was not successful.

Four men grabbed her and dragged her into the bushes at the side of the road. They tore off her only fancy dress and repeatedly raped her for over an hour. When they finished, they slapped her around and left her in the dirt: bruised, bloody, and naked. A horrific end to what had been a happy birthday.

Gabriela picked herself up after the men had gone and staggered the rest of the way home. Every part of her body was strained and sore from the struggle. She stayed in bed for four days, then burned her beautiful dress, and didn't go back to town until after Josefina came to check on her three weeks after they'd celebrated her birthday.

Gabriela knew the men worked for Quintana because she'd seen them in town many times and had heard people refer to them as "Quintana's men." She never told anyone what happened to her because she knew she would have been killed.

The hate had been growing in her for five years when she heard the explosions to the south and then saw two soldiers heading her way through the trees at the edge of her field. She started to run for the house when something stopped her. They were not Mexican soldiers. Their uniforms were different. These men were Americans. She'd seen men and uniforms that looked like that in *The Hurt Locker*: a movie her father took her to when they were in Guaymas visiting relatives. She stopped., turned, and waved the men toward her.

Luke and Chuck saw Gabriela waving and froze. They'd been spotted. Who was that woman? And why was she waving at them? Or *was* she waving at them? They knew Quintana's men were closing in from behind, so they crouched low and looked around but didn't see anyone else in the area.

Gabriela shouted, "Americanos, ven"—Americans, come.

The men knew enough Spanish to know she'd identified them as Americans and was asking them to come to her. They looked at one another, and Chuck said, "What do ya think?"

"She looks friendly and already knows we're Americans. Let's see what she wants."

Remaining hypervigilant, they stepped out of the woods and hurried across the pasture where chickens pecked at the ground, and two goats grazed on the deep grass. They slowed as they approached the girl.

Luke said, "Do you speak English?"

"Yes, but not too good."

"What do you want?"

"I see helicopter going around. Nobody has helicopter but Quintana. Then I hear guns and explosions. I think you here to get Quintana, so I help."

The distant sound of men shouting and the slapping of helicopter blades rose from the trees to the south.

Gabriela ran toward the house and said, "Come. You hide in my house. I show you."

Luke and Chuck ran after her as the whir of the chopper grew louder.

Gabriela rushed through the door, latched it once the men were in, and started dragging a large wooden table off a colorful, woven rug. She pulled back the rug and pointed to a square trapdoor cut into the plank wood floor and said, "Hurry. Go down. You be safe."

The helicopter was hovering directly above the cabin; it's whirling blades pressing air hard against the roof and throwing debris around the windows. The sound of voices intensified as the pursuing thugs crossed the clearing in front of the house.

Gabriela closed the hatch as Chuck's head cleared the floor. The sound of boots pounding the ground escalated as the professional killers drew near. She pulled the rug over the portal and inched the heavy table back onto the rug. She ran to the sink and pretended to wash dishes as the first assassin burst through the door, springing the latch and causing her to drop a plate. It shattered at her feet as she spun around.

Three men entered the cabin carrying weapons and raced toward her. Gabriela fell back against the sink and raised her hands to protect her face. She recognized one of the men as the first one who'd raped her on her nineteenth birthday. Fear and hate melded in her mind.

The men had neatly trimmed, black hair that was disheveled from pursuing the snipers. A hand with thick fingers and hairy knuckles grabbed Gabriela by the throat, and the gravelly voice behind it said, "Have you seen any men come through here?"

Gabriela tried to speak but no sound came out. The hand had cut off her air, so she shook her head as best she could while the human vice kept her locked in a death grip. Stars flashed before her eyes, and she was about to pass out when the goon relaxed his hold, and a deep breath filled her lungs. The man gave her a hard slap, and she fell to the floor. He held a gun on her while his two associates searched the small cabin. The men outside checked the barn and surrounding area.

Out of the corner of her eye, Gabriela saw that one corner of the rug under the table was turned up. She hadn't noticed it in her haste to hide the soldiers and give the appearance that it was an ordinary day. She looked away so as not to attract attention to the rug.

24

COLBY CHUCKLED AS he sat at his desk watching the action unfold in real-time on his computer. He'd just seen Luke and Chuck take out a drone and a helicopter as they made their way back to the extraction zone.

His chuckling stopped, and the smile on his face drooped as Luke stepped out from the rocks and into the clearing. Lines of static began to dance across the screen, and the image froze with Luke in mid-stride. A moment later, Luke took another jerky step as Chuck appeared from the rocky shelter. More static lines raced up and down the screen, and the image froze again. Luke and Chuck advanced a few more discontinuous steps before the static obliterated the image, and the screen went dark.

Colby's fist slammed down on the desk.

"What the hell?"

He frantically tapped on computer keys, but the screen remained blank. He clicked on another program, and the screen lit up. His computer wasn't the problem.

Colby grabbed the SATCOM10 satellite phone that linked him to the snipers and typed a text to Luke. *Are you OK?* An error message popped up on the screen. *Unable to send.* He typed the same message to Chuck and got the same error response.

"Damn it!"

He picked up his landline and punched in the code for the satellite command center. The call was answered on the first ring.

"This is Statler."

"Ah, just the man I want to talk to. It's Colby. What's going on with the communications satellite? I've lost GOVMAP and cell contact with my men."

"The satellite just went down. NASA notified us three days ago of a huge coronal mass ejection. It's the largest such ejection from the sun ever observed. We rotated the satellite into a defensive posture to enable it to take the hit with little or no damage. Unfortunately, we're in a high geosynchronous orbit, so we're very susceptible to these blasts. Apparently, one or more components have been damaged by high-energy particles that were able to penetrate the satellite. We're working to diagnose the problem and get it fixed as soon as possible."

"Damn. I've got men in the field that are in danger. I need to be able to communicate with them. Now."

"I understand. We're doing everything we can as fast as we can. Hopefully, you'll see it back up soon."

"Thanks. I know you're giving it your all."

Colby hung up, then put in a call to the director.

"This is Hewitt."

"It's Dan. I hate to bother you, but I need you to come down here ASAP. Operation Wolf Hunt is in trouble."

"I'm on my way."

Two minutes later, Director Hewitt entered Colby's office. "What's up?"

"All communication with our boys in Mexico is down."

"What?!"

"Satellite Command tells me a CME has knocked out the satellite. They're working to get it back up but don't know how long it'll take."

"Shit! What's going on down there? Where are we?"

"My last contact was about ten minutes ago. They were just moving out after taking down a drone and a helicopter. Several heavily armed men were about three-quarters of a mile to their rear and closing in fast."

"God forbid they're captured, or worse yet, killed. Can you imagine the hell that would cause? U.S. snipers entering Mexico without its government's approval to take out Mexican citizens. Even if they are scum of the earth."

"It's too soon to panic. Luke and Chuck are the best we've got, and they know how to evade capture. Besides, they don't have any ID on them, there are no names, labels, serial numbers, or other identifying marks on any of their clothing or gear. The weapons could have come from anywhere, and the satellite phones are useless without the codes."

"I hope you're right. Let's keep this to ourselves for now. The president has enough on his plate. Call me as soon as communication is back."

"Will do."

Hewitt left the room, and Colby resumed punching computer keys and trying to get the satellite phone to respond. He tried to remain calm, but the furrows in his forehead indicated he was less than successful. This mission was his baby. It had to succeed.

25

LUKE AND CHUCK stood in total darkness with their weapons pointed at the trapdoor above. The muffled sound of heavy boots and a threatening voice permeated the silence of the root cellar as something hit the floor with a loud thud. The high-pitched yelp that followed confirmed it was Gabriela. Then silence.

Chuck shot Luke a questioning look.

In a whisper, Luke said, "We'll never get that door open without being shot. She pulled the table over it."

Chuck nodded.

"There's nothin' we can do now but wait 'til they clear out."

Chuck nodded again.

The muted sound of heavy boots hitting the plank floor could be heard as two men raced into the cabin. An excited voice yelled, "They were here. Two men were here."

The man who'd slapped Gabriela held up a hand and said, "Whoa. Whoa. How do you know they where here?"

"I see tracks. In the field there are fresh tracks. Boot prints of two men and sandal prints of a small woman all together in the dirt. But the tracks disappear in the grass."

All eyes turned to Gabriela's feet. Her feet were small, and she was wearing sandals.

The fat hand that had choked Gabriela grabbed her by the hair and pulled her into a sitting position. Clinging to her hair, the man knelt and thrust his scarred, hairy face to within an inch of her nose. His breath smelled of garlic, whiskey, and stale cigarettes. The same smell she remembered from the time he'd raped her.

"Is that true, whore? Did you meet two men in your field?"

Wincing with pain as tears streaked her cheeks, Gabriela said, "No."

The man smacked her face with a blow that brought bright flashes of light to her eyes. Her lip split, and blood began to flow from her nose. An involuntary shriek exploded from her lungs as the hand drew back and smashed into her ear, causing sound to deaden.

The man screamed, "God dammit, you bitch. You're lying. Where are they?"

Gabriela's vision blurred. Images of angry men staring at her went in and out of focus. She could hear laughter but didn't know where it was coming from or if it was just her imagination. She tried to speak, but her mouth felt broken, and her tongue wouldn't move. Then everything went black.

The man pushed Gabriela to the floor, stood, pulled out his phone, and punched in a number. When the call was answered, he said, "Diego. We're at the González place. Two men have been here with Gabriela. They're gone but can't be far away. Send the helicopter and any men you can spare." He listened to Diego's response, then ended the call.

"Alright, listen up. You seven men spread out and head north. They can't be very far. I'll wait here for Diego. He's going to round up the four men on leave in Gato Grande and have them search the town. I'll join you after Diego picks up this slut."

The men took off at a run, fanning out to the east

and west. Eduardo Muñoz, the man with fat hands, paced from the door to the windows to make sure nobody snuck up on him. Luke and Chuck could hear the floor-deadened footfalls of his heavy boots, but there was nothing they could do because the rug and table covering the trapdoor prevented the element of surprise.

Gabriela began to regain consciousness. One eye fluttered open, revealing a fuzzy image of a man pacing back and forth. She licked her lips. The taste of blood permeated her mouth. Her gut knotted, and she sucked in an involuntary breath when she remembered the soldiers in her cellar. Fortunately, Muñoz didn't hear her. Her mind flashed on the upturned corner of the rug, and she tried to move her head to find it, but nothing happened, her strength was gone, and she slipped back into darkness.

26

DIEGO PEREZ SPRINTED from his office, yelling at Francisco Aguilar's pilot as he ran. "Grab one of my men and get that bird off the ground. Head north and start searching about two miles from here. Go all the way to the border if you have to. The two assassins are headed north on foot. Go!"

The pilot ran toward the helicopter. The guard nearest the chopper shouldered his AK-47 and rushed after him. Thirty seconds later the engine whined, and the blades began to turn. Three minutes after their rumps were in the seats, the skids were in the sky. The aircraft rose and sped north, almost clipping the guard turret on top of the house.

Perez raced to his truck, stopped, and waved his arms at Javier Abarca in the turret. He cupped his hands around his mouth and shouted, "You're the only one here. Don't let anyone you don't recognize get near the house. I'll be back within the hour."

Abarca gave a thumbs-up.

Perez jumped in his truck, unholstered his gun, and set it on the seat next to him. A cloud of dust obscured the truck as it sped toward Gato Grande. He flew through the small town and slid to a stop outside El Granero. The people on the street turned and stared. He grabbed his gun and ran inside the bar. Three of Quintana's men sat at a far table playing poker and drinking beer. They jerked their heads toward the door as Perez burst in. The men knew something was up because Perez was always calm, even in dicey situations. They jumped up and rushed to Perez as spilt beer dripped off the table and poker chips bounced across the floor.

The first man to reach Perez said, "What's up, boss?"

He filled them in on the details and said, "Where's Pablo?"

One of the men said, "With the prostitute."

Perez knew he was referring to Juana Jiménez. She was the only woman in Gato Grande who, at one time or another, had serviced all of Quintana's men, including the big man himself. He looked at the man with the long handlebar mustache and said, "Raúl, you and Gerardo head out. Search every building in town starting at the north end. Stay together. These men are dangerous." Looking at the third man, he said, "Fredo, come with me to get Pablo."

Raúl and Gerardo sprinted up the street as Perez and Fredo jumped in the truck and raced to the small shack at the west edge of town they all knew so well. Perez pushed open the door to the shack and saw Pablo's hairy backside. Pablo was bending Juana over the table in front of him and thrusting his hips forward and back, forward and back, forward and back. Except for her feet, Juana was completely hidden by Pablo's huge girth. His guttural grunts, the banging of the table against the wall, and Juana's high-pitched squeals prevented him from hearing the door open.

Perez shouted, "Pablo."

Juana let out a pain-edged shriek as Pablo whipped around and pointed his gun at the door before realizing who was standing there.

Perez said, "Drop the gun, Pablo. Both of them. Get dressed and get your ass out here. Now." He turned and went back out the door.

Pablo pulled up his jeans, retrieved his shirt from the floor, and dashed to the door without looking back at Juana. Juana pulled her dress back down as she turned around and hollered, "Hey, give me the money." He ignored her and slammed the door behind him. Juana shouted, "Dumbass! Don't come back."

Something shattered against the inside of the door as Pablo stepped into the sunlight. Perez looked at him and said, "Go with Fredo. He'll fill you in."

Fredo and Pablo hurried toward the south end of town. Perez sped back through town, sliding around curves and throwing up gravel as slack-jawed townsfolk watched the scene unfold. He made a hard right, almost skidding into a taco cart, and headed up the dirt road to the González place.

Gabriela was sitting in a chair with her elbows on her knees and holding her head in her hands when Perez walked through the door. Now two of the men who had ruined her nineteenth birthday were in her home. She looked up and tried to focus her vision.

Muñoz was sitting on the edge of the table, his legs crossed, smoking a cigarette. He stood when Perez entered. A helicopter could be heard sweeping over the treetops to the north.

"Did you send the men north?"

"Yes, Diego. They spread out east and west and are working their way north." With a quick jerk of his head toward Gabriela, Muñoz continued, "This bitch met with the killers. We searched the house and the barn. They're not here. She knows where they are."

Perez bolted to Gabriela, grabbed her by her hair, and whipped her head back. Pain shot through her neck and down her spine. Terror filled her eyes as a drop of blood trickled from her nose and stained her blouse.

"Is that true, you dirty dog? Huh?"

Gabriela stared into Perez's evil eyes. A slight smile turned one corner of her mouth as hate trumped fear. Then a glob of blood-infused saliva flew from her mouth and splattered across his face.

Perez's fist instinctively drew back and smashed into Gabriela's head, knocking her to the floor, and dislodging one of her teeth. The tooth skittered across the plank floor and came to rest against the far wall. Her cheek was red and broken. She was out cold.

Perez turned to Muñoz and said, "Go. Join the others. I'll take care of this one."

Muñoz retrieved his rifle from the back of the chair and ran out the door. Perez walked to the sink and splashed water on his face then moved to the lump of still flesh on the floor. He stood over Gabriela, sneering down at her motionless form. He grabbed one of her arms, and with one quick motion, picked her up and flung her over his shoulder.

On the way to his truck, Perez said, more to himself than to Gabriela, "I remember you well, Ms. González. It's been a while. I'm looking forward to getting to know you again." A low, raspy laugh dripped from his mouth. "All of you." He opened the door to his truck and tossed her in.

27

THE DIMINISHING THUD of boots was followed by the rumble of a truck engine that quickly faded to thundering silence. Luke and Chuck stood in the dark, weapons at the ready, and barely breathing as they tried to discern every nuanced sound from above. After several minutes of no sound except the soft inhalation and exhalation of their own lungs, Luke sucked in a breath and turned on his flashlight. The sudden burst of light shattered the darkened cellar, causing the men to squint.

Luke whispered, "I think we're clear. I'm gonna try to get this door open."

Chuck nodded.

Luke stepped up the ladder until his shoulder was pressed hard against the door. He pushed with everything he had, but the door barely moved. He tried again with similar results.

"Hey, Chuck. Give me a hand."

Chuck squeezed up the steps. Both men put their backs to the task and began slamming into the door. Each coordinated strike resulted in the purchase of a little more space between the floor and door. Five minutes of backbreaking labor raised the bottom edge of the door above the floor enough for Luke to wedge his WK Belt Knife into the gap and cut the rug. He pushed the door open and entered the warm air of the cabin. Chuck followed. Sun streamed in the open cabin door, illuminating the myriad dust motes dancing in the light, and pointing to a bloody tooth near the far wall.

Chuck saw the tooth and a small pool of blood on the floor near the kitchen sink and said, "Oh, my God. That poor girl."

"Yeah. We gotta do something. Those monsters will kill her. She helped us, and we gotta return the favor."

Chuck nodded.

Luke pulled out his cellphone, punched in Colby's number, and put the phone to his ear. Nothing. There was no ringtone. The phone was dead. He lowered the phone from his ear and looked at the screen. "What the hell?" He disconnected the call and punched in the number again. Nothing. They were cut off.

Luke said, "We're on our own, man. The phone's dead."

"Shit."

"We heard that truck pull out. Odds are they're taking her back to the compound. They're looking for us north of here, so we shouldn't have any trouble going back as long as we stay clear of the helicopter."

"Let's do it. We can deal with getting out of here once we've got her."

Luke agreed and walked to the door, staying out of the sunlight in case some of the lackeys had stayed behind to keep an eye on the place. Pressed against the wall to the left of the door, he scanned the visible surroundings, and not seeing anyone, stepped out. He motioned for Chuck to go right as he moved left. Both men sidled along the building while visually sweeping the nearby barn and field. Each man checked his side of the cabin and surrounding area for any sign of the thugs. Not seeing anyone, the men quickly moved to the barn and confirmed there were no surprises inside.

Luke tried again to contact Colby, but the call didn't

go through. He said, "Chuck, see if you can get ahold of Colby. It might be my phone."

Chuck entered Colby's number but didn't get a ringtone. He said, "Nothing, man. It must be the satellite or something on Colby's end."

"Well, at least we can access the topo map on the phone. That should help get us back to the ranch."

They studied the map to determine the best route to take and moved out, keeping to the trees and protected areas as much as possible. The trek back was uneventful, as expected. The helicopter kept searching to the north, and no other goons were encountered. Thirty minutes later they were back at their original firing position.

Luke pointed to an area of soft dirt and said, "They've been through here. There's a set of boot prints crossing the spot where we camped. Looks like they kept moving and didn't stop."

"I see that. Guess it pays to police brass and sweep the ground."

Both men dropped to a prone position, crawled to a spot with a clear view of the hacienda below, and scoped the area with binoculars. The bodies were still lying where they dropped. Everyone had either hurried north in pursuit of the snipers or were keeping a vigilant lookout for further trouble: too busy to tend to the dead. A flock of ravens had spotted the easy pickings and were hoping from body to body, pecking at exposed flesh. One appeared to have removed Quintana's left eyeball and was perched on his face while attempting to break it into bite-sized pieces. Maria Sandoval opened the back door and waved a broom at the black carrion-eaters. She was too afraid to get closer to her lifeless boss. The birds would fly a few feet and return to their meal when the door closed.

The man in the turret atop the house kept a close watch on the open space surrounding the property and occasionally trained his binoculars on the nearby mountains. He seemed nervous and kept jerking his head from side to side so as not to miss a potential threat.

Luke noticed the barn and the white pickup parked near the door. He turned his attention to the only visible window and adjusted the focus. He could clearly see the back of a woman's head. She had long, straight black hair and appeared to be tied to a chair. The material covering her shoulders matched the dress Gabriela had been wearing. A man kept circling her while pointing a gun at her head.

"Gabriela's in the barn."

Chuck turned his binos to the window and said, "That's definitely her."

"We've got to get her before that beast hurts her."

"Roger that."

28

LUKE'S PHONE VIBRATED, and he pulled it from his pocket. It was Colby. He punched ACCEPT, put the phone to his ear, and said, "What the hell happened to you?"

"The satellite went down, but we're back. What are you doing? You're supposed to be back at the extraction zone, but GPS has you at your initial firing position. Why? The chopper at Whiley is hot and waiting for the word to get you."

"Long story. But the short version is that a woman helped us evade the goons that were tailing us. Now they've got her here at the compound and will probably kill her if we don't intervene. That's not going to happen."

"You can't jeopardize this mission and risk exposing it to anyone outside the few of us involved. The president will have your hides. Get your asses back to the extraction point, now. That's an order."

"With all due respect, sir, when we're on a mission, we call the shots as best we can given the circumstances. And we're not leaving this woman in harms way."

"Damn it, Luke."

"Sir, I'd appreciate it if you'd keep tracking us live and give us a heads up if the helicopter is returning or any of the ground goons get too close. We'll contact you when we've got the girl. Right now, it looks like the place is quiet. Other than Quintana's staff and his mistress, there are only two of his thugs in the area. No one is out of the house except the armed guards. The rest of them are hunkered down inside and too afraid to venture out."

"The agency does not sanction what you're doing. You're putting the president and the country in a perilous position. If you screw up, there will be hell to pay."

"We won't."

Luke disconnected the call and pocketed the phone.

"Well, Colby's pissed."

"I figured he would be."

"Is the gorilla still in the barn with Gabriela?"

"Yeah. Nothing's changed there."

Luke put the binos to his eyes, made a sweep of the area, and said, "Looks like the biggest threat is Turretman. I think we should take him out and then move down."

"Agreed."

Luke secured the buttstock of his rifle against his shoulder, put his eye to the scope, and said, "Call it."

"Temperature here is seventy-four degrees. Should be about seventy-five or six at the turret. Breeze out of the west at two miles an hour. Relative humidity steady at fifty percent. Barometric pressure is 29.21 inches. Our altitude is 2,600 feet, and we're 234 feet above the target area. We're 2,602 yards from the edge of the pool nearest the house, the back of the house is another twelve yards beyond that, and the closest side of the turret is 2,626 yards."

"Got it. What's going on in the barn?"

"Nothing's changed."

"Ok, here we go."

Luke took several deep breaths and slowly exhaled. When his lungs emptied for the fifth time, his body stilled, and he slowly applied pressure on the trigger.

The supersonic bullet tore the air, and a reverberating boom bounced through the valley. Luke kept his eye on the scope and hoped Gabriela's tormentor didn't hear it. In a heartbeat, a red dot appeared in the center of Turretman's forehead as the back of his head painted the hacienda's roof.

Chuck said, "Bingo."

Luke swung his rifle around to the barn window while keeping his eye glued to the scope. The goon was still circling Gabriela. He didn't hear the sonic boom. That was a plus.

Luke said, "No problem at the barn. What's happening at the house?"

"Don't think they heard. Nobody has come out. The mistress came to the window for a minute in obvious distress. I guess loss of the lavish lifestyle is hitting her pretty hard."

Luke and Chuck started down the hill, keeping to the rocks and trees as much as possible, crouching low, and maintaining an eye on the barn. An occasional muffled scream from Gabriela split the otherwise serene afternoon. The snipers picked up their pace after each chilling outburst. They had to get to her fast before her captor lost his patience and decided to do more than circle her and intermittently punch her face.

29

PEREZ GRIPPED A thick piece of rope as he circled the diminutive woman slumped on the chair before him. Her eyes were closed, head bent to her shoulder, and mouth agape as blood dripped from her nose and cheek onto her blouse and torn white skirt.

"Wake up, bitch. Talk to me."

Perez grabbed a can from a work bench and filled it at the sink. Water sloshed over the sides and puddled on the floor as he walked back to Gabriela. He flung the water in her face, soaking her blouse and skirt. Her head jerked up and her eyes flew open as she gasped for breath. She wasn't wearing a bra, and the outline of her nipples combined with the adrenaline of violence aroused Perez. However, the urgency of the situation quickly quelled his craving.

The rope bit into Gabriela's arm, drawing blood as Perez vented his rage.

Her cry caused Luke and Chuck to quicken their descent.

Perez grabbed her throat and squeezed. He pressed his mouth against her ear and whispered, "You will tell me where they are, or I will kill you."

The grip loosened, and Gabriela sucked in air.

Perez stared down at her as the evil shot from his eyes. He turned, looked back, pointed a finger in her face, and said, "Don't go anywhere you pig. I'll be right back. You better have an answer for me because you won't get another chance."

Perez left the barn and headed to the house. He had

to pee. The day was warm, and the black carrion-eaters, multiplied in number, continued to circle the cabana, shattering the silence with loud squawks and fighting over tasty morsels of human flesh. Something didn't feel right. Perez glanced up at the turret—where was Abarca? He cupped his hands around his mouth and shouted, "Hey, Javier." No response. "Javier, goddammit, what are you doing?" Nothing.

Perez jogged to the house. That sonofabitch better not be sleeping. I'll take his balls. He jerked the patio door open with such force the glass cracked. Maria Sandoval was standing in the doorway to the kitchen. Terror etched her face as mascara-colored tears painted her cheeks.

"Where's Javier?"

"I don't know."

Perez darted past her and hit the stairs to the turret at a full run. He saw it as his head cleared the roofline; splotches of red and pieces of bone dotted the roof. Javier was doing a backbend over the turret wall. What remained of his head rested on the surrounding platform. A rictal grin belied dead eyes. What the hell? They're back.

Perez sprinted to the turret, slipping on a patch of red slime and landing on his butt. A crimson blob bloomed on his pants.

A pair of binoculars lay on the platform next to Javier's head—or what remained of it—the strap still wrapped around his neck. Perez grabbed Javier's nose and lifted the remaining head to free the strap. An eyeball flopped back into the detritus of brain. Despite his hardened exterior and the number of dead people he had seen, the sight of his friend's decimated head caused him to flinch.

Perez wiped the bloody binocular strap on Javier's shirt, dropped it over his head, and stepped into the turret. He did a slow 360 as he scanned the surrounding meadow and trees. Nothing. He did it again and again, each time searching higher up the mountains to the north. They had to be there somewhere. Based on Javier's wounds and the position of his body, the shot had come from the north. He pulled out his satellite phone to alert the helicopter before remembering the boss's chopper had been shot down. The only one still flying belonged to Bardales, and he didn't have phone numbers for his men. Damn.

Perez sent a group text to his men, informing them about Javier and telling them to direct their search back toward the compound. He hoped at least some of them would have line of sight to the satellite. If not, they wouldn't get the message. He picked up the binoculars and continued doing 360s of the area, focusing most of his attention to the north.

Something moved in the trees directly in front of him. Perez fixed his gaze on the spot. What the hell was that? It happened too fast for him to see what it was, but something definitely moved. He let the binoculars drop to his chest and moved to the .50 cal machine gun. He homed in on the spot through the gun's scope and placed his finger on the trigger. A small brown patch disappeared into the brush. Perez squeezed the trigger, his adrenaline pumping, and let thirty rounds fly in less time than it takes to inhale. Branches, leaves, and dirt exploded, causing a massive dust cloud. When the air cleared, a five-point set of antlers lay on the ground.

30

THE SOUND OF .50 cal rounds slicing the air and slamming into trees, rock, and dirt caused Luke and Chuck to dive behind an outcropping of rock. Fifty yards to the left, a cloud of debris floated on the breeze as aftershocks reverberated through the valley. They hadn't been the target.

Chuck said, "As many times as I've heard that sound, it still gives me the chills every time."

"Copy that."

Luke peered over the rock and raised his binoculars. He could see the .50 cal in the turret with its barrel pointing in their direction. A man stood next to it, field glasses pressed to his eyes, and staring back at their location. Luke ducked out of sight and waited, expecting to see the ground explode around them. Seconds passed. Nothing. They hadn't been spotted.

Chuck said, "What'd you see?"

"There's a guy in the turret scoping out the area. I don't think he saw me, or he'd have opened up on us by now."

Luke slowly raised his head above the top of the rock and focused on the turret. The man appeared to be turning circles while searching the surrounding forest. He stopped turning and concentrated on a ridge to the east.

Luke sat back down and said, "He seems to be looking in all directions. If we can work our way through the trees to the left, we should be able to drop down to the edge of the meadow behind the barn without being seen. When he's looking south, we can run across the open space to the barn."

"Sounds like a plan. Let's do it."

Luke inched his way to the edge of the boulder, and Chuck followed. He did a quick check of the turret and said, "He's still focused to the east. Let's do it on three."

"Got it."

Without taking his eyes off Turretman, Luke counted, "One, two, three."

They were both up and running toward the trees, hoping they didn't attract the goon's attention. Chuck slipped on some loose stones and put his hand to the ground to keep from going down. The twenty yards of open space seemed to go on forever, but they made it. The spot they were aiming for was another seventy-five yards through the trees, then down a shallow valley to the edge of the meadow where the barn provided protection from Turretman's view.

Tall pines kept them hidden, except for a few open areas that required a quick turret check. They passed the place where .50 cal bullets had shredded the vegetation and earth. A beautiful five-point buck lay in pieces. Its body ripped apart by the unforgiving rounds.

The narrow valley was steep and made up of dry, powder-like dirt that, when disturbed, would be lifted by the slightest breeze and scattered above the trees. Luke and Chuck crouched low so as not to be seen. They moved slow, with deliberate steps, to avoid raising a dust cloud that could give away their location. It took longer to descend the eighty-foot-long valley than to traverse seventy-five yards through the trees. But they finally reached the meadow.

Luke and Chuck both raised their binoculars and scanned the open space, far tree line, and barn. The area was clear. The turret was not visible. Only the far edge of the house and one outbuilding could be seen from their location. There were no windows in the exposed part of the house, and the outbuilding appeared unoccupied.

They were about to move out when the distant chop of a helicopter broke the silence. They took cover in thick brush at the edge of the meadow.

Luke said, "Great! Just what we need."

The helicopter came in from the north, flew directly over them, circled the compound, and landed on the helipad on the opposite side of the barn. It was partially visible from the snipers' location. Two men got out with the engine running. A man dressed in black with an AK-47 slung over his shoulder ran to a bush and relieved himself. The other man walked to the fuel tank, dragged the hose to the chopper, and began hot refueling.

A man ran up to the guy refueling, waving his arms, and pointing back toward the house. It was Turretman.

Luke and Chuck could hear the man shouting but couldn't understand what he was saying over the buzz of the engine. It was obvious he was telling the chopper pilot about Javier Abarca. Turretman pointed to the north, made a motion with his arms that said hurry up and get going, then turned and ran back toward the house.

The pilot returned the fuel hose to the tank, the bush irrigator zipped his pants, both men got back in the chopper, and a minute later, the bird was airborne. It made a quick circle of the meadow and disappeared to the north.

31

LUKE SAID, "MOVE to the right until you can see the turret. If Turretman goes back to his post, we should be able to get to the barn undetected.

Chuck stepped out and crouched low so as not to be seen above the brush.

Luke kept his eyes on the exposed corner of the house and outbuilding for any sign of the only thug believed to be on the property. It was vacant except for a large tabby cat, unfazed by the surrounding death, and napping on a patio chair.

Chuck reached a spot where he could see the turret and checked it with his binoculars. It was empty except for the body of the former tenant draped over the back wall. He looked at Luke and shook his head. He turned to work his was back to Luke when he caught movement out of the corner of his eye. Chuck stopped and looked back at the turret. Turretman had returned and was reaching for his binoculars. Chuck motioned to Luke, pointed at the turret, and mouthed, "He's back."

Luke gave a thumbs-up and did a final check of the surrounding area.

Chuck moved into position next to Luke.

Luke said, "You ready?"

"Ready."

Both men crouched low and ran to rear of the barn. With their backs pressed against the wall, they did a visual sweep of the tree line they'd just left. All clear.

Luke peered around the corner of the barn to confirm they could reach the window, and Gabriella, without being seen from the turret. It was clear.

The men worked their way toward the window while staying alert to the surrounding open area. When he reached the edge of the window, Luke raised his hand to let Chuck know he was stopping. He glanced in the window and saw Gabriella slumped in the chair. Her hands and feet were tied. She wasn't moving.

Chuck kept his eyes on the open area while Luke used the butt of his rifle to break out the window. Gabriela's head jerked up, and she let out a scream as the window shattered, but the terror in her eyes eased when she saw Luke's face. The sound of breaking glass may not have reached the turret, but Gabriela's shrill scream surely did.

Luke put his finger to his mouth to silence her and said, "Let's move." He crawled through the window with Chuck right behind him.

Gabriela cry-whispered, "thank you, thank you, thank you," over and over as tears stained her cheeks.

Luke rushed to her side and began to untie her as Chuck kept his eyes and revolver on the door and window.

Luke had her hands and one foot free when the pounding of boots could be heard approaching the door. Luke kneeled on one knee, drew is revolver, and faced the window. Chuck dropped to a knee and faced the door.

The slap of boots hitting the ground grew louder. Gabriela tried to shield herself with the chair as best she could with one foot still tied when the door burst open. Perez froze, his eyes wide, conveying a mixture of shock and fear. A bullet tore through his heart before the synapses of his brain finished firing the message as to what was happening. His body flew back and slammed against the wall as he slid to the floor.

Chuck moved forward and checked Perez's pulse. There was none. He moved back to assist Luke and get Gabriela out of the barn.

Luke cut the rope anchoring Gabriela to the chair, lifted her up off the floor, and moved to the window. Chuck peered out at the open space to ensure it was clear, then exited the barn. Luke handed Gabriela to Chuck through the opening and crawled out.

Luke looked at Gabriela and said, "Are you able to walk?"

"Yes. My body is sore, but I can do it."

The men stayed alert to their surroundings as the three of them moved to the back of the barn, across the open meadow, and back into the trees. They stopped behind a boulder. Luke handed Gabriela an energy bar and offered her water from his camelback. She devoured the bar and continued to drink until Luke retrieved the bite valve from her.

Luke said, "Don't drink too much or you might cramp up. You can drink more later."

"OK. Thank you."

They started to move when Luke's phone vibrated. He took it out of his pocket and saw it was a message from Colby. He tapped on the message. *I've been watching you. Well done! Now get the hell out of there. The chopper is about 3 klicks due north. Some ground goons have reached the extraction zone. New pick up location. Head to N30°20'19" and W110°09'48". I'll send the chopper when I see you're close. Good luck.*

Luke typed *Roger*, pressed SEND, and typed in the new pick up coordinates. The new location was four klicks north-east, over a mountain ridge, and in a valley near Arizpe, Mexico. He turned to Gabriela and said,

"We've got to walk about four kilometers over the mountains. Can you do that?"

"Yes, but what are you going to do with me?"

"You're not safe here. We'll take you with us to the United States and figure it out from there. Are you OK with that?"

"Oh, yes, yes. Thank you."

32

DIRECTOR HEWITT SAT on the couch in Colby's office as a Cheshire cat grin exposed his teeth. Colby had just filled him in on the latest Operation Wolf Hunt developments.

"That's fantastic, Don. Better than we could have imagined. What do we know about the girl?"

"Not much, other than she helped Luke and Chuck evade Quintana's men. She risked her life doing it."

"How long before they're in the air heading back?"

"They're leaving the compound area now. The extraction point is four klicks north-east through the mountains. Assuming the girl can walk on her own, and they don't encounter any resistance, they should be there in about two hours."

"Great. Let's get the president on the horn and give him the good news."

Hewitt punched in the number for the White House and waited to get patched through to the Oval Office. The president picked up.

"Don, good to hear from you. What's up?"

"Thank you, Mr. President. I wanted to update you on Operation Wolf Hunt."

"Great. How's it going?"

"It couldn't be better, sir."

Hewitt spent five minutes giving President Mitchell the details of the mission.

"Oh my, that's wonderful news. It's about time those cartel bastards were sent a powerful message. Good work, Don. And pass on my congratulations to

Colby. His orchestration was flawless."

"Thank you, sir. I'll let him know."

The president disconnected the call.

Hewitt hung up. "The president said congratulations. He thinks you did a terrific job. So do I."

"Thanks, Don."

"I'm going to head back to my office and let you wrap this thing up. Let me know if anything changes. And congratulations again. You may be taking over my office when I retire."

"I hope you plan to stick around awhile. The agents really like you."

Hewitt smiled and closed the door behind him.

Colby turned to the satellite tracking on his cell to watch the action unfold. The helicopter and men on the ground were still to the north. The chopper was crisscrossing the valley and moving south. Luke, Chuck, and the girl were about two-hundred yards east of where he last saw them. Things were looking good. He sent a text to Luke. *Chopper and men still to the north. Chopper crisscrossing the valley and moving south.*

Colby pulled up his directory and searched for Colonel Bradford's number. He was the commander of Fort Whiley. He entered the number on his landline while continuing to watch the operation in Mexico.

Bradford answered on the third ring. "This is Bradford."

"Colonel, it's Dan Colby at Langley."

"Yes, Dan, I've been expecting you to call. What's up?"

"I need you to get agents Donnelly and Gomez saddled up and ready to move. I'll call you when we're ready for them to take off. Should be in about an hour and a half. A new pick up zone has been established at coordinates N30°20'19" and W110°09'48". It's in a valley a half mile north of Arizpe, Mexico. Have them stay low in the valleys and out of sight."

"Will do. The bird is fueled and ready to go. They can be ready to lift off in ten minutes."

"Thanks, Colonel. Have 'em stand by. I'll give you a call."

Colby hung up and returned to the action on his cell.

33

LUKE AND PARTY exited the trees at the edge of an expansive and steep shale field. Straight ahead, a fifty-foot-high rock wall blocked their way. They couldn't go directly across, and going down was not possible because the wall ended at an abrupt drop-off. Up was the only option.

The soles of Gabriela's huarache sandals were worn smooth, making it hard for her to gain traction on the loose rock. Luke held her arm to keep her from falling. The going was slow, and mini slides were triggered every few steps. Mini they could handle, but a major slide could be devastating. With no trees or large rocks for cover, they were exposed and vulnerable to attack from the air. There was no sound except the fall of their feet and the clatter of rock hitting rock. But given the mountainous terrain, a helicopter could appear with little warning.

Gabriela was breathing hard, but she didn't complain. They reached an area with more solid footing, and Luke stopped. He offered her water, and she took a few swallows. She could have drunk more but remembered Luke's warning about cramps. She handed Luke the drink tube, and they moved on.

Twenty feet from the top of the shale field and the cover of trees, they heard the slap of rotor blades. Luke tightened his grip on Gabriela's arm and started to run. Gabriela lost her footing and went down. Luke's grip saved her from a hard fall, but she twisted her ankle and let out a muffled cry. The buzz of the chopper grew louder. It was on the other side of the ridge and almost on them.

Luke and Chuck got in position with one knee on the ground. Chuck pulled up the grenade launcher, and Luke shouldered his rifle. They scanned the sky in the direction of the sound. Gabriela pushed her body close to Luke and buried her head in her hands. Where was it? The sound seemed to remain in one place. It was hovering. Had it spotted them?

After a tense moment, the sound began to recede. It was moving south, back toward the compound.

Luke turned to Gabriela and said, "How's your ankle? Can you walk?"

"It hurts, but not too bad. I think I can make it."

Luke looked at her ankle and saw it was beginning to swell. He reached in his pack and pulled out an Ace bandage. Placing her leg on his thigh, he wrapped the ankle, careful not to cut off her circulation.

"How's that?"

"Good. Thank you."

"Not too tight?"

"No. Is good."

Luke shouldered his rifle and helped Gabriela to her feet. She put her weight on it and said, "It's OK. I can keep going."

Chuck got up, shouldered the grenade launcher and said, "Let's get the hell outta here."

"Roger that."

They made it to the top of the slope and back into the safety of the trees. Luke continued to grip Gabriela's arm to help take the weight off her injured ankle.

Chuck said, "I need to take a quick break. Mother Nature has been calling, and I can't hang up on her again." He walked into the trees and disappeared behind a large boulder. Luke gave Gabriela another sip of water and took one himself. Thirty seconds later, Chuck stepped into view still buttoning his fly.

Luke's phone vibrated. It was a message from Colby. *That was close. Chopper is on other side of the valley and moving south. Two men are a kilometer north and working your way. Hey, Chuck, I could see Willy from the satellite. Very impressive!* Luke smiled and closed the message.

Chuck said, "What's up?"

"Colby could see your willy from space. You the man."

"Ha-ha. Very funny."

"No, seriously, that's what he said."

Chuck punched Luke's shoulder.

"He also said we've got two unfriendlies a klick north and moving our way."

Luke pulled up the interactive topo map on his phone, studied it for a moment, and said, "Looks like our best bet is to move about a hundred yards east and follow the valley toward the extraction zone."

They followed an animal trail trough the brush, up a slight rise, and down into a shallow valley where large oak and pine trees provided cover. It was easygoing compared to the shale field. Gabriela was able to walk unassisted.

The valley was peaceful. A welcome change from the events of the past few days. A gentle breeze cooled the valley as puffy white clouds paraded across the powder blue sky. Distant raven chatter provided a counterpoint to the silence as red-tailed hawks rode the thermals. Luke and Chuck remained vigilant despite the calm. The illusion of tranquility had been shattered without warning too many times during tours in the

Middle East.

As they approached the head of the valley, the sound of men's voices brought them to a halt. The men were close. Luke looked at Gabriela and put a finger to his lips. She nodded. Chuck tapped Luke's shoulder and pointed to a cluster of rabbitbrush ten feet off the trail. They moved to the brush and lay prone behind it.

The voices grew louder. Luke and Chuck drew their revolvers and pointed them toward the trail. The sound of shoes scrapping dirt could be heard as two men wearing jeans and guayabera shirts came into view. Not the thugs. Just two locals out enjoying the day. The trio relaxed and waited for the men to pass.

Back on the trail, Luke pulled out his topo map to check their location. They were south-west of Arizpe and a kilometer from the extraction zone. The terrain ahead was flat with lots of tree cover. Barring any unexpected delays, and keeping the pace slow for Gabriela, they should reach their destination in twenty minutes.

Luke's phone vibrated with a message from Colby. *I'm sending helo now. Should be there shortly after you arrive. Stay safe.*

34

THE EXTRACTION POINT was a small clearing surrounded by chaparral and piñon pines. A shallow stream edged the perimeter. Luke pointed to a large rock shaded by pine trees and said, "Let's wait over there. Our ride should be here soon." They picked a flat spot and sat down.

Chuck opened his pack, pulled out his last MRE, and said, "I don't know about you, but I'm starving. Man, these things have never looked so good."

Luke agreed and pulled out his last meal. Gabriela's eyes grew wide at the sight of food. It was her first taste of Uncle Sam's rations.

The whir of a helicopter could be heard to the north. Luke and Chuck policed the area, shouldered their gear, and helped Gabriela to her feet. The bird landed and kept the blades turning. The three of them crouched low and ran to the open door. Luke lifted Gabriela into the cabin and climbed in behind her. Chuck followed. They strapped in as the chopper lifted, cleared the trees, and banked north.

Gabriela grabbed Luke's arm as they picked up speed. It was her first helicopter ride. She looked at Luke, smiled, and mouthed, "Thank you."

Luke smiled back and nodded.

Agent Donnelly got on the horn and said, "Good to see you boys again. I see you brought a friend."

Luke looked at Donnelly and said, "Yeah, this is Gabriela. She's been a great help to us."

Donnelly said, "Hey, Gabriela. Nice to have you on

board."

"Thank you."

Gabriela stared out of the window as the landscape flew past. Her land, her people, the only home she'd ever known. Would she see it again? And Josefina, her best friend. She didn't get to tell her goodbye. Josefina would wonder what happened to her and worry. Would they ever share a laugh together again? Oh, and her animals. What would happen to them? Would Josefina come looking for her and take care of the animals? A tear worked its way down her cheek. She wiped it away with the back of her hand. Her thoughts turned to America, the United States. Her parents had often talked about it when she was a little girl. They dreamed of going there one day for a better life—and now, she was doing it. A fragile smile etched her mouth.

The helicopter banked left and set down on the pad at Fort Whiley. It was over. They'd made it.

A shiny Gulfstream G650 was parked on the tarmac next to them, its engines running.

Luke and Chuck shook hands with Donnelly and Gomez and thanked them for the lift. Luke grabbed his gear and got out first. He turned, lifted Gabriela to the ground, and said, "Welcome to the United States." She looked into his eyes, her lips trembling, tears welling up in her eyes, and threw her arms around his neck. Chuck gave Luke a thumbs up and jumped to the ground.

The flight back to Andrews Air Force Base was uneventful. Luke and Chuck fell asleep shortly after the wheels were up. Gabriela couldn't sleep. She leaned her head against the window and watched the sun set. It had been a long, traumatic day, and her entire body hurt. She was exhausted, but the excitement of what had happened and where she was kept her awake. The land below was the promised land. The land her parents had hoped to one day call home. Then fear crept into her thoughts. Would she fit in? How would she live? Where would she live? A frown creased her brow.

It was night when they landed, but a full moon lit up the base. Gabriela stepped off the airstairs, went down on her knees, and place both of her hands on the tarmac. She bowed her head and was silent. When she lifted her head, Luke helped her up.

Colby walked toward them, all smiles. He shook hands with the men, congratulated them on a job well done, then put his hands on Gabriela's shoulders. He looked her in the eye and said, "Young lady, thank you. You saved our mission. You're a hero. Thank you."

Gabriela smiled and looked down as blood rushed to her cheeks.

Colby turned to Luke and Chuck and said, "You all must be beat. Let me take your back to Langley. Get a good night's sleep, and we'll debrief in the morning."

35

LUKE KNOCKED ON Gabriela's door at 8:00 a.m., and they walked to the restaurant for breakfast. She'd been up since five thinking about the past few days and wondering about her new life. They joined Chuck who was seated in a booth next to the window.

After breakfast, they met with Colby in his office.

Coby said, "Have a seat," as he moved to the chair behind his desk. "I want to thank you again for a job well done. The outcome has exceeded all expectations. I can tell you the president is very pleased, and he has arranged to meet with you later today."

Gabriela's mouth dropped open.

Colby said, "Yes, Gabriela, President Mitchell has specifically asked to meet you."

Her hand moved to her mouth as tears blurred her vision.

Colby continued, "I don't know how much you know about our mission in Mexico, but it's very important that you not discuss it with anyone. Can you do that for me?"

"Oh, yes, yes. Is no problem."

"Good. Now, if you don't mind, I'd like to ask you to wait in the conference room at the end of the hall while I talk with Luke and Chuck."

Gabriela stood and said, "OK."

Colby walked her down the hall and returned to his office. Director Hewitt joined them, and the next hour and a half was spent debriefing Luke and Chuck.

Director Hewitt left, and Colby brought Gabriela

back to his office. She returned to her seat, and Colby sat at his desk.

Colby said, "Gabriela, I'd like to know what you want to do now. Do you want to stay in the United States, or would you rather go back to Mexico?"

"Oh, stay ... if it's OK."

"It's definitely OK. I just want to make sure it's what you want."

"Yes, it's what I want."

"Great. The president has requested that a green card be issued to you as soon as possible. That will allow you to live and work in the United States on a permanent basis."

Gabriela smiled and said, "Thank you."

Colby said, "I believe, given what happened in Mexico, it would be in your best interest to assume a new identity, take a new name. Because the cartels will look for you, and they have very long arms. Are you OK with that?"

"Oh, yes. I understand."

"Do you have a name in mind? Think about it because it's the name that will be on your green card, and the name you will use from now on."

Gabriela thought about it for a moment and said, "I do have a name I like. Gloria Gomez. Both names start with *g* like my name now. Gabriela González."

"Gloria Gomez it is. Gabri ... Gloria do you have any relatives or friends in the US where you can stay?"

"No. Nobody."

Luke cut in and said, "She can come with me to Colorado and stay with my mother until she decides what she wants to do. I'm sure my mom can use her around the house, and I can use some help with my business." He looked at Gloria and said, "That is if you want to do that."

Gloria looked at Luke with a sparkle in her eyes and said, "Thank you, Mister Luke. I'd like that."

Colby said, "Perfect." He reached for his phone and continued, "I'm going to have the department photographer come and take your picture for the green card. Is that OK?"

"Yes, but I don't look so good. Maybe I can use the restroom first?"

"Of course. It'll take him a while to get up here anyway. Do you remember how to get to the ladies' room?"

"Yes." Gloria stood and walked to the ladies' room at the end of the hall. She splashed water on her face and used a paper towel to dry. She straightened the collar on her dress and tried to press out some wrinkles with her hand. Her hair was tangled but looked much better after running her fingers through it several times. She stared at herself in the mirror and smiled at the thought of living in the United States and fulfilling her parents' dream.

The photographer was waiting when she returned to Colby's office. He had her stand against the white wall and look at the top of the camera. She didn't know if she should smile but did. The moment was too happy not to.

Colby turned to the photographer and said, "Can you download that and send it to my computer when you get back to the office?"

"Will do." He folded his tripod and left the office.

Colby turned to Gloria and said, "I'll get the green card forms filled out today and send the package to the card processing plant in Kentucky. I'll have it expedited, so you should have your green card in a week or two. You'll also get a social security number so you can work and open a bank account."

"Thank you so much."

Colby said, "Gloria, it's very important that you not tell any family or friends your new name or where you're living. I know it's going to be hard, but don't communicate with anyone from your past. No one knows about this other than President Mitchell, Director Hewitt, Luke, Chuck, and me. Can you do that?"

"I understand. Yes, I can do it."

"Your meeting with the president is at four. Your car will meet you in front of the main building at two-thirty. You'll be driven back to Andrews Air Force Base after the meeting, and the jet will take you home. In the meantime, make yourselves at home around here. Any questions?"

Gloria said, "Yes, I have a questions. I don't have clothes good enough to meet the president. Is there a place for me to get a dress?"

"Good point. Thanks for reminding me. I knew two days ago that the president wanted to meet you all. Since I already had your sizes from when we ordered your fatigues for the mission, I took the liberty of acquiring suits for you gentlemen. And, Gloria, I guessed your size based on the pictures I saw of you and got a dress for you. I hope it fits and you like it."

Gloria said, "Oh, thank you. You're very kind."

"I'll have the clothes delivered to your rooms. Should be there in twenty minutes."

Luke and Chuck both said, "Thank you, sir."

"All right. That wraps it up at this end. I'll see you at the car before you leave."

36

A BLACK SUBURBAN was waiting in front of the building when they arrived. Director Hewitt and Colby were already there. Two burly agents were at the car, both in suits, one behind the wheel, the other holding the door open.

Director Hewitt stepped forward to greet them, and as he shook their hands, said, "I want to thank you all again for a job well done. You've done a great service for our country, Mexico, and the world."

Luke and Chuck said, "Thank you, sir." Gloria smiled and looked down. They got in the car, and the agent shut the door.

Colby walked up and tapped on the window. As it rolled down, he said, "Get some R and R. You deserve it. I'll be in touch the next time your services are needed."

Luke said, "Thank you, sir, but I'm not sure there's going to be a next time. This mission was grueling. Life in small-town Colorado is a lot calmer and safer."

Colby smiled, turned, and as he walked away, said, "See ya soon."

The window rolled up as the car started down the drive and out of the compound. Next stop, the White House.

37

THE SUBURBAN LEFT 1000 Colonial Farm Road and circled the compound on the access road to the George Washington Memorial Parkway. They exited onto the Curtis Memorial Parkway and crossed over the Potomac River on the Theodore Roosevelt Bridge. They drove down E Street Expressway and made a left onto 18th Street NW. They passed the World Bank complex and turned right onto H Street NW. Gloria was all eyes as the SUV rolled past the massive buildings of DC. She'd never seen anything like it. The suburban continued past Lafayette Square, turned right, and work its way to East Executive Avenue NW. They stopped for the security check, then drove onto the White House grounds and parked outside the East Wing, where an escort led them to a waiting room. Gloria tried to look in every direction at once as they moved through the massive building.

Chuck sat in an overstuffed chair, fiddled with his tie, wiped the perspiration from his upper lip, and said, "Wow, this is a first."

Luke said, "Yeah, we've had some pretty incredible experiences, but this is right up there."

"No kidding."

Gloria said, "Is this where the president lives?"

Luke said, "This is where he lives and works."

Gloria's eyes were wide as she surveyed the room and said, "I never dreamed."

Luke said, "Me neither."

A white light on the phone near the door blinked,

and the escort lifted the receiver. He said, "OK," hung up, and motioned to the three guests. "The president will see you now. Please, follow me." He stepped into the hall and held the door for the guests.

Chuck stood and whipped his hands on his pant legs. Luke offered his hand to Gloria to help her up. They moved into the hall and walked beside the escort.

As they passed into the West Wing, the escort said, "Just a couple of things when meeting the president. Address him as Mr. President. Don't offer your hand to him. Let him offer his hand to you. And don't sit until he offers you a seat."

Luke and Chuck said, "OK."

Gloria nodded.

The escort said, "Any questions?"

All three guests said, "No."

When they reached the door to the Oval Office, the escort knocked twice and opened the door. He stepped in and held the door for the guests. As they entered, the escort said, "Mr. President, may I present Gloria Gomez, Luke Garrett, and Chuck Reagan?"

President Mitchell stood, stepped out from behind his desk, walked toward them, and said, "Welcome. I'm so pleased to meet you." He put his left hand on Luke's shoulder and his right hand on Chuck's shoulder and continued with, "Gentlemen, you have done a great service for our country both as SEALs and now with this latest mission. Thank you. You're true patriots."

Luke and Chuck both said, "Thank you, Mr. President."

The president stepped over to Gloria and took both of her hands in his. He looked deep into her eyes and said, "Ms. Gomez, you're a very brave young lady. You risked your life to keep these men out of harm's way. They may not be here today if you hadn't intervened, and it could have been a real embarrassment for the United States. Thank you."

Too afraid to respond, Gloria smiled and nodded.

President Mitchell asked them to sit and took a seat across from them. He offered them tea and coffee, and they spent five minutes chatting and getting to know one another.

The president stood and motioned for his guests to follow him as he moved to his desk. He removed three flat, square, brown boxes from his desk drawer and slid them to the opposite side of the desk. He looked at Luke, Chuck, and Gloria and said, "In honor of your bravery and service to the United States, I'd like to present each of you with the Presidential Medal of Freedom."

Luke and Chuck looked stunned. Gloria looked down at the boxes and back up at the president. She'd never heard of the Medal of Freedom.

The president opened the boxes, took out a medal, and one-by-one fastened a medal around each guest's neck, and said, "Thank you for your service."

The Chief Official White House Photographer snapped a picture as each medal was given and then took a group picture with the president.

They talked for a couple of minutes, and the president walked them to the door. President Mitchell took Gloria's hands in his for the second time and said, "Ms. Gomez, I sincerely hope you will consider remaining in the United States and becoming a citizen. The freedom we enjoy depends on people like you."

"Thank you, Mr. President."

The escort opened the door and walked them out of

the building.

EPILOGUE

THE JET LIFTED off the runway, banked left, and started its climb to forty-one thousand feet. The White House could be seen in the distance out of the right side of the plane. It looked so small.

Gloria pressed her face to the window and watched the city fade away until thin clouds erased the view. She sat back in her seat and closed her eyes. She thought about Josefina, her parents, the farm, and her small village. The only life she'd ever known. Sadness over what she was leaving behind, and excitement at the thought of a future in the United States, danced a pas de deux through her mind. An image of the handsome man sitting next to her brought a smile to her face. Luke. She wondered if he fit into her future.

Luke opened the box he held in his lap. He touched the silver eagle attached to the blue ribbon, ran his finger around the white star, and counted the thirteen stars in the center. He thought about his career as a SEAL, all the people he'd killed, and wondered if it had all been for the greater good. He hoped so. Small-town Colorado, the mountains, clear streams, and pine trees are what he looked forward to now. He looked at the slender, brown hands of the woman next to him. He studied her face, the flawless brown skin, the full lips, and the shinny black hair. He'd never seen a more beautiful woman.

Chuck reclined his seat and fell asleep at thirty-five thousand feet.

Free Copy of The Visitor

Visit www.stephenrossauthor.com for a FREE copy of my suspense/thriller short story "THE VISITOR" and Notice of New Books/Sales

~THE VISITOR SYNOPSIS~

The morning broke like every other in the small Midwestern town of Porterville: quiet and peaceful. It's a farming community where church basement potlucks and Sunday drives in the country are the main sources of entertainment. Nothing much ever happened there until the arrival of the visitor.

Eighty-six-year-old resident Ima Plummer could not have imagined how her day would end when she awoke that fateful Wednesday.

You won't want to stop reading.

About the Author

Stephen Ross practiced law until retiring in 2017. His first novella, MEMOIR FROM HELL, received the 2019 Reader Views Reviewers Choice Award. It was praised by Reader Views as "realistic and genuine … the ending is dramatic and haunting," and by author Anthony Avina as "an emotionally charged novel that needs to be read." Stephen's other work includes, POWER LUST, a legal and political thriller set in California, and a supernatural thriller, THE VISITOR. Born in Iowa and raised in Nebraska, Stephen now lives in San Diego, California. When he's not writing, he enjoys reading, hiking, camping, and movies. He can be reached via his website at www.stephenrossauthor.com, on Facebook at www.facebook.com/stephenrosswriter, on LinkedIn at www.linkedin.com/in/stephen-ross-639114105, and on Twitter at www.twitter.com/stephenross48.

Also By Stephen Ross